MEANT FOR HER

MEANT
—FOR—
HER

AMY GAMET

Copyright © 2012 Amy Gamet
Printed in the United States of America

ALL RIGHTS RESERVED.
This book contains material protected under International and Federal Copyright Laws and Treaties. Any unauthorized reprint or use of this material is prohibited. No part of this book may be reproduced or transmitted in any form or by any means, electronic or mechanical, including photocopying, recording, or by any information storage and retrieval system without express written permission from the author / publisher.

For Brian,
who always believed I could do it.

Special thanks to Laura Davis,
Deyôn Waller, Pam Kaptein,
Melissa Sharp, Dale Richards, and Paul Richards.

—1—

HANK JARED WAS running.

Four miles in, he hit his stride. Heavy metal music poured from his headphones, drowning out all but the rhythmic beating of his shoes on the pavement. The neighborhood around him was upscale and well-manicured, with stately rolling lawns and automatic sprinkler systems that wet his dark hair and tan, bronzed skin.

His physical conditioning was evident in the controlled swish of air in and out of his lungs, the defined muscles of his calves and thighs flexing in synch with the pumping of his arms. He checked his watch. Plenty of time to get back and pack before his flight.

Five days before Christmas, and it feels like the middle of May.

He had been in Florida nearly a month, working on a case for Admiral Barstow. While Hank enjoyed the sunshine and novelty of swimming in December, his amusement turned to irritation when he saw his first palm tree covered in Christmas lights.

He needed a blue spruce, and he needed it quickly.

By nightfall he'd be in the Adirondacks. His mouth formed an unconscious smile at the thought of his destination. His little sister was getting married on Christmas Eve, and the whole family was gathering at his mother's house for the event.

I'll be walking her down the aisle.

The thought brought with it the faintest grief, a wave by now so familiar Hank simply accepted its crest. It had been more than five years since their father passed away.

Ray Jared had been a strong, kind man with a boisterous sense of humor, a love of the outdoors and a deep dedication to family. Kelly's wedding made their father's absence as tangible as a shadow where sunlight once shined, and Hank was both honored and saddened to stand in the spot his father should have occupied.

The residential neighborhood ended in a cul-de-sac, lined on one side with evergreens. The hedges obscured a ten-foot high chain link fence, a small opening in the foliage marking an entrance to another space beyond.

Hank slowed to a walk, retrieving a plastic card from his running pack. He slid it through a small card reader on a steel post, the gate unlocking with a metallic click.

Acres of turf surrounded what looked like a business complex. The newest field office of the U.S. Navy was nothing if not discreet. Hank enrolled right after college, having always dreamed of a career in the armed forces.

The military was his life.

His breathing slowly returning to normal, he dug in his pack for his cell phone and dialed the familiar numbers.

"Don't be mad, mom," he said when she answered. "But I'm not going to be able to make it." He sounded devastated to his own ears.

"Hank William Jared, that wasn't funny when you were ten, and it sure as hell isn't funny now."

He chuckled. "It's a little funny."

"It might be a little funny if the caterer hadn't double booked."

"You're kidding."

"Nope. And it would have been downright hilarious if the wedding bands had arrived at the jewelers."

Maybe he picked the wrong day to joke with his mother.

"I can fix this, Mom."

"How are you going to fix it?"

"I'll treat for pizza."

"That's very helpful, dear."

"I am a helper, you know."

"Yes, you are. What time does your flight get in? I have a to-do list here with your name on it."

Hank was sure she had an actual piece of paper that said HANK across the top. With three children and a family business to run, his mother had a great deal of experience delegating responsibility. "Three-thirty. Who's picking me up?"

"Ron. He and Kelly have been playing chauffer all week." Kelly's fiancé had seemed like a nice enough guy the few times Hank had met him, but he was happy to hear that Ron was playing taxi driver so they'd have a chance to talk. Without his father, it seemed like his responsibility to give Ron the third degree.

Kelly met him on an airplane when she was on her way home from college for Christmas break two years ago. Hank got the feeling there was more to that story, and he intended to get the whole truth from Ron before the wedding.

"No worries, Mom, I'm on my way..." Hank was interrupted by a call waiting beep. He checked the caller ID and frowned.

"Mom, I have to take this."

"Work?"

"Yes."

"Don't answer it, Hank. Bad things come in threes and we only have two."

"I have to."

"I know you do," she sighed. "Call me later."

Hank clicked over to the incoming call.

"What can I do for you, Admiral?"

"I'VE GOT A nasty virus. Almost a third of the company is infected." Julie Trueblood rested her forehead on her fingers as she leaned over her desk.

"Are you going to be able to make it for Christmas?"

Julie never planned on making it to her aunt's house, though she had plenty of time to fit it in before her trip with Greg. She spun her chair around and watched fat snow flakes falling at an alarming rate over the city of Boston.

"Even if I clean up all the computers, I'm afraid I'd need a fleet of tiny reindeer to pull my sleigh and get me out of the city. What's your weather like?"

"A little snow, I think. We have a few inches already."

Julie knew that 'a little snow' to her aunt might well be enough to put the entire northeast into a state of emergency. Aunt Gwen was pushing hard for Julie to make it out to Vermont this year, and had extended an open invitation for the long weekend. It was a solid three-hour drive in good weather, and this was anything but.

"I don't know. Let me run and see what progress I can make on this virus. I'll give you a call in a couple of hours," she said, instantly regretting that she hadn't simply said no.

"Alright, Jules. Best of luck. I can't wait to see you."

Julie cringed into the receiver. "Bye, Gwen."

She turned her attention to the computer in front of her and sighed at the work ahead. Firewalls and anti-virus software could only do so much. Someone was always out to make a better virus that could slip in under the radar and wreak havoc on a stranger's computer. Or in this case, more than eighty of Systex Corporation's desktops.

Her morning had been spent identifying the virus and downloading the fix. Now she needed to spend ten minutes on each machine to get it working again. Picking up the phone, she dialed Becky's extension.

"Becky's House of Beauty."

"I need help cleaning up a virus. It's going to kill the rest of the day."

"Yee haw! I'll be right in."

Julie shook her head and smiled as she replaced the receiver. Becky had been her roommate at MIT, where they both majored in computer science—Julie with a double major in math, Becky with a minor in social work. Becky was good enough at what she did to have Julie's job, but she lacked the finesse necessary to climb the corporate ladder.

If it bothered Becky that she worked for Julie, she didn't let on.

"Okay, what are we up against?" asked Becky, walking into Julie's office without knocking.

"Eighty-one machines, ten minutes to fix each one."

Becky's eyes lit and she smiled widely. "I'd say the company should buy us lunch."

"Deal." Julie checked her watch. "Let's get through two-thirds of them before we break, though."

THE CRIME SCENE was easy to find.

The Orange Palm Motel had a turquoise pool, white lounge chairs, and a string of tangerine doors— the overly bright pattern now violently interrupted by a swath of blackened siding. The fire had buckled the roof shingles, blown out the window, and left gray swirling murals of soot and ash on neighboring units.

Hotel guests stood in the parking lot or sat on cars, watching the drama being played out before them like theatergoers staring at a stage. Police milled about behind yellow tape as firemen and EMTs packed up their gear.

There was no one to rescue here.

Hank ducked under the tape and strode toward the charred motel room, flipping open his badge as he was approached by a uniformed officer. Hank shook his head when the other man raised his hand and walked away, knowing the cop hadn't gotten a good look at Hank's badge.

That was too easy.

He replaced it in his pocket and withdrew a pair of vinyl gloves, pulling them on before confidently slipping into the room.

The darkness was near complete, the smells of burned wood and plastic clinging to the wet air. There was another odor as well, and Hank knew at once the room had been occupied. He withdrew a slim flashlight from his pocket and began searching for the body.

A beam of light shined on him.

"Detective Johnson, Jacksonville P.D."

He turned. "U.S. Navy Lieutenant Hank Jared."

"Navy?"

"Navy."

Johnson lowered his beam to Hank's chest. "Is our victim military?"

"The Navy has an interest in this case."

"An interest in this case," Johnson repeated. "Is that a no?"

"I didn't say that."

"The victim's in the bathtub," said Johnson. "Unidentified male, unless you're going to tell me who he is." He shined the light back at Hank. "You going to tell me?"

"What makes you think I know?"

"You're here. There must be a reason for that. I wouldn't even know who to call, but the U.S. Navy is here, and I'm trying to figure out why."

"Let me know if you come up with anything."

Hank headed for the bathroom, carefully making his way through the debris and pooled water on the floor.

The body was terribly burned. "He die in the fire?"

"Coroner's on his way."

Hank shined his beam in Johnson's eyes, and the other man sighed heavily.

"He was shot."

"Accelerant?"

"The arson dog caught a whiff of something."

"Anything else interesting?"

Johnson nodded. "A key to a safe deposit box near the body. A ring. No other personal items or identification, though they might have been fuel for the fire. Every car in the lot is accounted for. The room was rented to one Mark Smith. Clerk doesn't remember him—checked in three days ago."

"You wouldn't mind if I came with you to check out that safe deposit box."

"Of course not, officer."

"I SWEAR, HE had to be six foot eight. Just massive,"

Becky stood up and mimed what looked like King Kong tromping over tiny buildings. "His shoulders barely fit through the door. Biceps like that guy on the Energy Pump commercial." She flexed her own shapely arms and flung her red hair backwards as she admired her small muscles.

"And so he walks up to me and says, 'Have dinner with me.' Just like that. Can you believe the arrogance?"

"I'm guessing you said yes."

"Heck yeah, I said yes! I practically threw myself at his feet and begged for him to be the father of my children right there in the bar! Then I decided I should wait until after our date just in case he was psychotic."

"Just in case."

"Right." The waiter appeared to refill their drinks.

"And?"

"And, what?"

"Did you go to dinner with him?"

"Gino's Via Abruzzi." She smacked her lips.

"And the man?"

She wrinkled her nose. "Too much baggage."

Julie turned to her Cobb salad, arranging one forkful with a tiny piece of chicken, a leaf of lettuce, bacon, and avocado.

"You're eating that salad like it's the last thing on earth you can control."

"Very insightful, Dr. Phil," said Julie as she dipped

the tip of her concoction in blue cheese dressing. "Anything else you'd like to analyze today?"

"How about your love life?"

Julie gave her a warning look.

"How is Greg?" Becky asked in an overly bright tone.

"He's good. Fine."

"Good. Fine."

Julie glared at her. "He asked me to go on a trip with him for Christmas." She knew better than to tell Becky that Gwen had invited her for the holiday, too.

"Really? Where to?"

"He didn't tell me." Julie hesitated before adding, "He bought the tickets as a surprise."

Becky slammed down the iced tea she'd been drinking. "Without asking you first?"

"Yes."

"You hate surprises! Doesn't he know how much you hate surprises?"

"I don't hate surprises!" Julie began making another perfect Cobb salad forkful as she spoke. "It's romantic. It's thoughtful."

"It's fan-tastic!"

Julie put down her fork with a loud clink on the table. "Say it."

"Nope. Everything's good. Fine."

"Just say it."

"Say what? That you're pretending to like the idea

of a mystery trip when we both know you'd rather have all the hair on your body pulled out by the root? Or that you're dating the most unappealing bachelor this side of the Mississippi because you don't want to be alone for Christmas?"

"Christmas doesn't have anything to do with it."

"Ah, but you concede my other point. The guy's a waste of plasma."

Julie could feel a headache beginning to throb in her left temple. Why was she having this conversation? "Why do you have such a problem with Greg?"

Becky took a long sip of her drink before answering. "He gives me the creeps." She bit down on a piece of ice. "And honestly, Jules? I don't think you like him any more than I do. Pretend it's January, sweetie. Let it go."

Julie knew she should defend her boyfriend, but nothing came to mind. How come nothing came to mind?

Because a waste of plasma is an apt description.

She used her fork to redistribute the chicken evenly over the surface of her salad. When had she decided that it was better to date someone she had no interest in than to be alone? It wasn't just Greg, he was just the latest in a continuous stream of guys she didn't even like. The kind of men who had always been attracted to her.

"You're right," said Julie.

Becky was halfway through a bite of her Philly steak sandwich and talked with her mouth full. "I am?"

"He's an ass."

Becky slammed the table with her open hand, getting the attention of several other diners. "That's what I'm talking about!"

"He annoys the absolute crap out of me."

"Amen, sister!"

"He talks about random, bizarre things. Invasive bamboo and the growth cycle of hair. I can tell you more about asphalt than you would ever want to know."

"Let it all out."

"When he touches me I want to pat his head and tell him to sit."

Becky snorted. "Please tell me you haven't slept with him."

"Ugh," Julie visibly shuddered. "His hands are wet. Not just damp, Becky. Wet. Always."

"Feel better?"

Julie turned sad eyes to her best friend in the world. "I wanted to like him," she said quietly.

"I know, sweetheart."

"I wanted to love him."

"Let's not get carried away."

Julie pulled out her cell phone and dialed before she could reconsider. "Greg, it's Julie. I'm not going to make the trip this weekend. We need to talk. Call me when you get this."

"I wonder where he was going to take you."

"Don't you dare."

"Oh, relax. You did the right thing." Becky took another bite, a string of cheese running from her mouth to the bun. "I'm just saying, someplace warm might be nice at Christmastime. Maybe a few palm trees."

MARIANNE JARED WAS standing in her large country kitchen making Christmas cookies en masse, holiday music playing in the background. With her daughter's wedding just days away, she was calming her nerves and preparing to feed the hungry crowd that would be descending.

She had the gingerbread men stacked up on cooling racks, and had just started blending butter and sugar for the next round when the phone rang.

"Hello."

"Hi, Ma."

She felt her stomach clench at his tone, and walked away from the stand mixer, leaving it running. "What's wrong?"

"I'm not going to be able to make it to the wedding, for real."

She brought her hand to her face and pinched the skin between her eyes, counting to five before trusting herself to speak. "Why not?"

"There's a case here in Jacksonville. Barstow insisted I handle it." He sighed heavily. "I'm so sorry, Ma. I can't get out of this one."

"Did you tell him you're scheduled for vacation? That's it's been on the books for months?"

"Of course I did. I even told him about the wedding." Hank cursed under his breath. "He was adamant. I'm so angry I could put my fist through a wall. Any of the investigators could handle this. There's no reason I have to do it."

She could hear the pain in his voice, knew it was genuine.

"Ma, if there's any way in hell I can make the ceremony, I will."

She nodded, staring at her feet. "We miss you."

"I miss you, too."

"Hank Jared is here to see you."

Julie didn't recognize the name. It was probably a vendor, though it struck her as odd that a sales rep would be doing cold calls the day before a holiday weekend. "I'll be right out."

As the Vice President of Technology for Systex Corporation, Julie was frequently the target of cold calls from salespeople working for computer companies.

She rounded the corner to the reception area and got her first look him. *Yes, Virginia, there is a Santa Claus.* He was considerably taller than her own five foot ten, with wavy dark brown hair, wide shoulders, and a presence that was totally masculine.

Julie felt butterflies stirring in her stomach and hoped she didn't make a fool out of herself. She was always uncomfortable talking to men who were more beautiful than she was. This guy was so far out of her league, she might trip over her own shoes.

"Mr. Jared. I'm Julie Trueblood. What can I do for you today?" The sweet smile on her face belied the pounding of her heart in her chest. He was even more attractive up close, with honeyed brown eyes and the lightest shadow of a beard on skin that looked tan from the sun.

"I'd like a few words with you, Ms. Trueblood."

"About what, exactly?"

Hank eyed the receptionist, who stared right back. "It's a personal matter."

She was hoping to skip out a little early today and had no intention of getting stuck with a sales rep for an hour. "What company do you represent?"

"The U.S. Navy."

The world around Julie froze for an instant, with the words hanging between them like the first gunshot of a battle. She remembered to breathe in, then out. She blinked her eyes.

"Come with me, Mr. Jared." She led the way from the lobby through a short hallway that connected to a longer corridor, feeling his presence behind her like a shadowy figure stalking her through a maze. Memories of other Navy officers assaulted her, panic rising in her chest with every step.

Julie motioned for him to enter the room before her, then locked the door and stepped behind her desk. "What can I do for you today?" she asked, her voice flat.

"I'm not sure." Hank leaned back in his chair and watched her. "Someone set fire to a motel room in Jacksonville, Florida yesterday morning."

Her brows drew together.

"The room was occupied at the time."

She flinched and looked away. "That's horrible."

"I flew up here this morning because I thought you might have some information about the case."

"Why would you think that? I don't even know anyone in Jacksonville."

"But you know someone in the Navy."

Her eyes slammed into his, and she knew she gave herself away. She raised an eyebrow and smiled at him without humor. "A friend from college is a Navy pilot."

"Is he."

"Yep. And there's always Richard Gere."

"Zack Mayo."

Julie rolled her eyes. "Whatever."

"The actor's name is Richard Gere, the character he played was Zack Mayo."

"You know what I meant."

"What I know is that you're messing with me, and I don't appreciate it."

Julie leaned forward on her desk. "I'm not messing with you. I don't know anyone in Jacksonville, and I haven't known anyone in the Navy in almost ten years."

"Who *did* you know in the Navy?"

Julie crossed her arms over her chest.

"I'll find out eventually, Ms. Trueblood."

"But you'll have to work for it, Mr. Jared. And that will please me immensely."

He held up a man's ring with a flush black stone. "Have you seen this before?"

Yes. Oh, God, yes. "No."

"You're lying to me."

"I'd like you to leave," she said, standing and crossing to the door.

"I'm not done yet." Hank reached for his briefcase. "There was a key to a safe deposit box inside that motel room. Inside, I found this."

He held up a single sheet of white paper, "JULIE X. TRUEBLOOD" scrawled in heavy black ink.

"Funny thing to include your middle initial. There are hundreds of Julie Truebloods in this country, did you know that?" He put the paper back into his briefcase. "Someone wanted to make sure we found you."

"How do I know you didn't make that yourself?"

"You don't. But that wasn't the only thing in the safe deposit box."

Hank handed her a yellow lined page torn from a legal pad. Four lines of scrambled text rushed along, without a nod toward spaces or punctuation. They defied interpretation, which hadn't stopped Hank from staring at them for the past twenty-four hours.

Julie lifted the paper between shaking hands.

"The safe deposit box was registered to John McDowell." Her eyes finally met his, her face contorting into a horrified frown.

"Do you know him, Julie?"

Her eyes filled as silent sobs racked her body. "Go. Please go."

Hank stepped forward, opening his arms to her, and she was drawn to the comfort he offered. She leaned against him, too distraught to care that he was a stranger, a Navy officer. She wept, inhaling the heady smell of him, his body heat palpable through the fine cotton of his dress shirt.

"Who is John McDowell?" he asked quietly. "Is that his ring?"

The pointed question turned the man from comforter to interrogator. She flew out of his arms, ashamed that she had let herself seek solace there.

"Get out of my office."

"Ms. Trueblood…"

"Get out of here right now or I'll call security and have you removed!"

He nodded and raised his hands in surrender, reaching into the pocket of his coat.

"Call me if you want to talk, or if you need help. Whoever hurt this man is still out there." He pulled out a business card and pointedly placed it on her desk. "I just want to help you, Julie."

Then he was gone.

2

THE EVENING LANDSCAPE glowed blue in the moonlight, as a silent rush of flurries fell in a continuous swirl onto the blanket of white below.

Inside, a freshly cut pine tree glowed with a single strand of white Christmas lights, its illuminated branches bare of ornamentation. Two dogs slept in front of a crackling fire, one small and gray, the other big and yellow and loudly snoring. Neither was disturbed by the low howling of the wind nor the clink of tools from the kitchen table.

Gwen Trueblood's art studio was pristine, with neatly kept wooden drawers and rows of labeled plastic containers. But it was a glorified closet, a staging area where she stored her supplies and prepared her materials. The kitchen was where she engaged her art, whether it be a bold pair of fused glass earrings or a loaf of fresh, crusty artisan bread.

Granite countertops mixed rich hues of gold with rusty reds and oranges in bold waves and specks. The cupboards were handcrafted of warm cherry with strong lines and careful moldings, their hardware a unique mixture of colored glass and sparkling metal that coordinated with the sunset colors of the granite around them.

A hefty island was surrounded on three sides by generous work areas, industrial appliances, and two oversized sinks. Pendant lights hung like jewelry, glittering in their display of brightly colored glass and dazzling metal. In the daytime the room would sparkle from the sunshine pouring in from the tall south-facing windows.

An impressive coffee maker and a craft kiln were displayed with equal prominence on the counters, along with a hand-woven basket filled with fresh fruit, an irregular loaf of golden-crusted bread, and a half-full bottle of red wine. Gwen was expecting company despite the weather, so she worked on a glass mobile and a rich pot roast at the same time. Both were for her niece.

She selected a deep purple from the stack of glass sheets before her, and worked to score it carefully before snapping the sheet into perfectly formed pieces. Beneath her hands, the glass became a series of graceful triangles that longed to twirl on metal strings.

In her mind's eye, Gwen could see Julie driving

through the snow, though the treacherous travel was not what concerned Gwen. Far more worrisome was the heavy heart she sensed in the woman at the wheel, and the simple reality of her destination. She knew that Julie would not come to Vermont unless something was terribly wrong.

She had invited Julie here, as she did every Christmas, hoping that her sister's daughter would come for a visit. But she understood more than anyone that Julie had her demons, and her reasons for staying away were not likely to change.

Pulling the pile of glass sheets onto her lap, Gwen sifted through them as she thought about Julie. Purple was the dominant color, but she could also feel red and sharp bits of yellow. She took the colors out of the pile and began to score the sheets into small shapes and skinny lines. Relying on her natural sense of balance and proportion, Gwen worked to create shapes that represented the emotions clamoring around her niece, then set them on top of the purple triangles in pleasing asymmetry.

As she completed each piece, she added a metal hook between the layers of glass and arranged them on the rack for firing. The pieces would fuse together in the kiln, creating one smooth surface that retained the separate colors. Then Gwen would combine the fused glass pieces with hammered brass and mirrors to create a mobile for her niece.

Gwen set the rack into the kiln and fired it up. The pieces of glass would slowly be transformed into their new shapes—reminiscent of the old, but stunning in their combinations. The high temperatures required for the metamorphosis meant that the pieces would not be cool enough to touch until morning. Gwen reflected that the process of change was often an arduous one, both in art and in life.

Turning her attention to the large copper pot simmering on the stove, she removed the lid and bent her head close to the soup to inhale its rich scent. It was not a fatted calf, but the intent was the same. Gwen was celebrating the arrival of her long lost niece, and she wanted everything to be special for her. Mentally she imagined that Julie was getting close, so she began to chop up the parsley and basil on a thick bamboo board. They would be added to the pot just before serving.

The ringing of the doorbell woke the dogs and set them to barking. Gwen smiled and rushed to answer the door, her joy at Julie's arrival somewhat tempered by her concern. She opened the door and a dense gust of icy wind entered the cozy house.

Upon seeing her aunt, Julie's half smile collapsed into a grimace. Gwen pulled her into the house as she shut the heavy door against the arctic air, bringing Julie straight into her arms for a tight squeeze. A stranger might have thought they were sisters rather than aunt and niece, separated by only ten years or so and equal in height and build.

"What's wrong, Julie?"

She choked on the words as they came out of her mouth. "My dad died."

There are a lot of freakin' Julie Truebloods.

This time, the X wasn't helping, either. Hank was sitting in a dark hotel room in downtown Boston, a laptop and a beer on the desk in front of him, trying to find the connection between the dead guy in the motel fire and his Julie Trueblood.

Well, not *his* exactly.

"She wanted me to work for it," he said to himself, trying various combinations of her name and the few facts he had in this case. It wasn't until he typed "Julie Trueblood Navy" that he was rewarded for his efforts.

NAVY COMMANDER JOHN MCDOWELL ACCUSED OF ESPIONAGE, VANISHES.

"Holy shit."

Hank's brow creased as he frantically scrolled down the screen, searching for Julie's name. What did she have to do with an infamous traitor?

"Gwen Trueblood, McDowell's sister-in-law, has been granted temporary guardianship of McDowell's minor daughter, Julie. The commander's wife, Mary McDowell, died of cancer ten months ago."

Julie Trueblood was Julie McDowell.

Hank had seen a 60 Minutes piece on the case years ago, though he never would have recognized the woman she had become. John McDowell was a cryptographer for the Navy, who passed the contents of secret messages on to Uzkapostan. He was single-handedly responsible for the sinking of the U.S.S. Dermody that killed eighty-eight soldiers.

If Systex knew about her background, she'd be fired faster than an arsonist at a fire station. Systex was a major manufacturer of information systems, with several substantial government contracts. No wonder she went by Trueblood.

He searched for "Julie McDowell Navy" and was rewarded with thousands of hits. Clicking on images, Hank's screen was transformed into a collage of photos taken around the time of the scandal. One black and white in particular caught his eye, a young Julie trying to get through a mob of reporters, her eyes wet, a backpack strap on her shoulder.

Hank wanted to throttle that photographer.

His cell phone rang and he checked the caller ID.

"Merry Christmas, man."

Chip Vandermead had been Hank's roommate in college. Hank called him occasionally when the Islanders played the Penguins, but Chip's position as an analyst with the NSA is what kept him on Hank's speed dial.

"How's Melody?"

"Pregnant."

"So you said. That's great."

"Twins."

"Oh, crap."

"We're going more with the, 'Isn't it wonderful?' approach, but 'Oh, crap' has crossed my mind."

"Sorry, man. That's awesome. Congratulations."

"She's due on Valentine's Day, but she's never going to make it. She's as big as a house." Hank heard a woman yelling in the background. "What? I'm not talking about you." He chuckled. "So, what's up? I know you didn't call just to wish me a Merry Christmas."

"I need a favor."

"Of course you do."

"I have an encrypted message, and I need to know what it says."

"Tell me about it."

"Four lines of text, Seventy-nine characters all together."

"Can't help you."

"What?"

"It's too short. Unless someone wanted you to be able to read it, and used a known cipher that's able to be read with a computer algorithm or something. Who wrote it?"

"Commander John McDowell."

"You're kidding."

"Not kidding."

"The man's a legend. Personally, I thought he was dead."

"He is now."

"What happened?"

"Somebody shot him, then set a fire to cover it up."

Chip whistled. "Where'd the message come from?"

"A safe deposit box. The key was at the scene." Hank looked at the hundreds of pictures of Julie on his computer screen as he talked. "I need to know what that message says, Chip."

"I can run it through the computer, but don't get your hopes up."

"Thanks. I owe you one."

"You owe me a hell of a lot more than one, Jared. Do you know anything else about this message? Sometimes it's the littlest thing that helps break a code."

Hank thought for a minute, wondering what might be relevant. "The only other thing in the safe deposit box was a sheet of paper that said Julie X. Trueblood. I already tracked her down. Looks like she's his daughter, going by her mother's maiden name."

"Okay. I'll see what I can find out."

JULIE WRAPPED THE sky blue terry bathrobe around

her warm, damp body and walked out of the bathroom, a cloud of steam following her into the much cooler bedroom. Her wet hair was piled on her head and wrapped in a pale yellow towel, just like the one she used to dry herself off out of the shower. Gwen had a masterful understanding of creature comforts, and Julie smelled of mint and rosemary from the decadent shampoo, soap and lotions her aunt provided.

Warm hardwood floors gave way to plush carpeting beneath her feet as Julie made her way to the window seat and sat down on its edge. She took in the familiar view below, the landscape's pristine blanket of snow shining bright in the late morning sunshine. A gently sloping yard bowed before rolling hills in the distance, and the horizon spoke of mountains tinted purple by the tilt of the earth itself.

Julie leaned forward and pressed her forehead to the cold glass, allowing her eyes to close in recognition of the peace she felt in this place.

This room had been hers when she lived with Gwen, and she acknowledged it for the haven that it was both then and now. It was ironic to be comforted by these walls after years of avoiding the solace they so freely afforded. Julie had not been here once in the time since college.

Vermont reminded Julie of the darkest time in her life—her own despair over her father's disappearance. Here lay the ashes from which she had risen like a phoenix, and only another fire could have brought her back again. In this place she was the daughter of a traitor, stalked by the media and villainized by the Navy officers who continued to interrogate Julie long after her father escaped their influence.

Her return to Vermont had been determined the moment Hark Jared set foot in her office. Last night, Gwen listened intently as Julie told her about the fire that killed her father. She thought of it now, picturing the scene as if she witnessed its deadly fingers reaching to destroy her ultimate hope—that her father would some day return to her and to his rightful place in her life.

Opening her eyes, Julie was surprised to realize that there were no tears on her face, as if the well of grief had simply gone dry from her great gulps at its waters in the last two days. She touched her cheeks with her hands and marveled at their normal texture, dry and soft.

The reality that life continues despite tragedy was both an odd comfort and a bad joke that rubbed at her and made her chafe on a spot that was already raw.

Julie had stumbled into bed last night after talking to Gwen until the wee hours of the morning. Now she looked around the familiar room and saw it had been transformed. The antique furniture that had been painted a bold coral when Julie lived here now matched the pale yellow of the fluffy towel on her head. Bed linens of turquoise and bright yellow toile seemed to hum in their bold contrast to the muted blue of the walls. A bulky duvet was wrapped in a lemony fabric that felt like the softest bunny, and the pineapples atop the four posts of the bed had been gloriously decorated in hammered gold and blue glass.

Walking to the bed, she again sank into its inviting depths. She pulled the duvet over her robed body and closed her eyes, wishing for the sleep that she suspected would not come.

She willed her mind to think of something else. An image of the sexy Navy officer filled her head. Hank Jared. Even his name was sexy. She remembered what he smelled like—pungent soap and something exquisitely male. Her knees almost buckled when her eyes had first locked with his.

A knock at the door disrupted her reverie. "Come in."

Gwen handed her the phone. "It's Becky."

"Hey, what's up?" said Julie.

"I'm at your place. I came to feed Sammy like you asked, and Jules, someone's been here."

"What do you mean?"

"I mean, someone broke into your condo. It's pretty bad. Your dresser drawers have all been dumped out onto the floor, and the kitchen cabinets are open and everything's messed up."

"Someone broke into my condo?" She sat upright

in bed. A cat meowed on the other end of the phone. "Is Sammy okay?"

"Yeah, he's fine. He was locked in a closet and none too happy about it. He's okay now."

"Did they steal anything?" In her mind, Julie ran through a list of her valuables, most of them electronics, and most of them with her on this trip.

"I don't see your laptop or your iPod."

"They're with me. Becky, do you think Greg..." Julie let her voice trail off, not wanting to say the words out loud.

"I know, he was my first thought, too. Was he upset when you dumped him?"

"He never called me back. I just figured he got the message and wanted to avoid the whole conversation."

"It looks like he was upset."

"Yeah. Looks like." Julie realized Gwen was watching her, her eyes questioning. "Someone broke into my condo and trashed the place." She choked on an unexpected sob as she said the words, covering her mouth with her hand.

Gwen sat and touched her shoulder. "That officer said you might be in danger."

"It's just some loser boyfriend I dumped last week, Gwen. Either that, or some neighborhood kids up to no good..."

"I don't think so, Julie." Julie looked into Gwen's eyes, and what she saw there sent a chill down her spine. Gwen had a sixth sense about some things, and Julie had learned long ago to listen when her aunt spoke with this quiet authority.

"Uh, oh," said Becky into Julie's ear.

"I feel a darkness. I don't want to scare you, but there's evil here." She held Julie's eyes as tightly as she held her hand, wishing to impart strength to her niece at this time. "Did the ex-boyfriend have a darkness about him?"

"I wouldn't say that," said Julie.

"Well, I would," chimed Becky. "Tell Gwen that I would, Jules. Tell her."

"He gave Becky the creeps."

"So maybe it is the boyfriend, then. Or it might have something to do with your father's murder."

That possibility was feeling very real to Julie.

"Perhaps it's time to call the Navy officer who came to see you in Boston. It will give you a chance to get a look at that encrypted message from the safe deposit box, too," said Gwen.

"I don't want to see the message."

Gwen turned exasperated eyes to her niece. "Your father finally wrote you a letter after all these years, and you're not even going to read it?"

JINGLE BELL ROCK played on the car radio, but Hank wasn't listening. A knot had settled in the valley between his shoulder blades, and he tried to stretch his arm across the steering wheel to release the tension. The lines on the pavement slid by in hypnotic straights and curves as his mind tried to make sense of the last several days.

Johnson had hit it out of the park before Hank even realized something was wrong. *Given what I know about this scene, I wouldn't even know who to call, but the U.S. Navy is here, and I'm trying to figure out why.*

Hank didn't like playing catch-up. Someone knew the body in the motel room was Commander McDowell before he was called to the scene like a puppet. Admiral Barstow had been the one to send Hank there, but that didn't necessarily mean he was the one pulling the strings.

Hank dialed his commanding officer.

Formidable and unconcerned with niceties, the admiral exerted his influence skillfully over those under his command. Hank was one of the few who remained unaffected by the other man's demeanor, and suspected he had earned the admiral's begrudging respect.

"What do you have for me?" said Barstow.

"The motel fire was deliberately set to cover up a murder, sir," said Hank.

"Whose murder?"

"It seems the body is that of Commander John McDowell."

The line was silent, and Hank resisted the urge to

speak to fill the void. If his suspicions were correct, the admiral was already well aware of who had died in that fire.

"What makes you believe the body is McDowell?"

Hank told him about the ring, the safe deposit box, Julie Trueblood and the cipher. "Dental x-rays were sent in for positive identification."

"A lot of good that will do."

"Sir?"

"All of McDowell's service records are gone, from his basic personnel file to the data from his last assignment," said the admiral. "Including his dental records."

Hank was stunned. It was no small feat to make someone's entire military existence disappear. "What happened to them?"

"They were deleted from our computer system, either by someone in the Navy with the clearance to do so, or by someone who hacked into that computer system."

"People can actually hack into the Navy's computers?"

"Computer gurus with exceptional code breaking knowledge and expertise," said the admiral. He pronounced guru like it had quotation marks around it. "Someone like McDowell's daughter."

"Is she that good?"

"McDowell was one of the best cryptologists the

Navy has ever seen, but the daughter was rumored to be some kind of prodigy. McDowell bragged she was better than he would ever be. Then she grew up and got herself a degree in mathematics and computer science."

"That's why the Navy kept interrogating her when her father disappeared. If she sympathized with him, she was a threat to national security just like he was."

"Yes. And it's why the Navy has kept tabs on her all these years, no matter what she wants to call herself."

Hank didn't allow himself to consider his next words. "You knew it was McDowell in that motel."

"We got an anonymous tip."

"An anonymous tip," Hank repeated. The sheer convenience of such a tip made it suspect.

"A voicemail left on my line. It said we'd find McDowell and his last secret."

"The message from the safe deposit box."

"Yes. Send me a copy of it."

"Yes, sir."

"And you get Julie Trueblood to decipher it, Jared. If anyone can, it's her."

"I'll see what I can do." As Hank hung up the phone, he steered his SUV onto the exit ramp. According to his GPS, he was less than half an hour from Gwen Trueblood's house in Vermont. He had been about to head to the airport for his flight back to

Jacksonville when Julie phoned and told him about the break-in. He had offered to come out, and she had quickly accepted.

It wasn't like Hank to keep things from his commanding officer.

"Sometimes, you've got to trust your gut," he said to himself.

3

As Hank stepped up to the front door of the unlit house, he had an uncomfortable feeling, like he had shown up for a party on the wrong day. He found it hard to believe no one was home after a personal invitation and a five hour drive.

Hank heard nothing when he rang the bell, so he knocked loudly on the door for good measure. He was rewarded with the barking of dogs who quickly came to the other side of the door.

Turning around, Hank surveyed his surroundings by the day's last light as he waited. The white farm house had a wide front porch with turned railings and a painted wood floor. A two-story barn loomed to the side of the garage, and distant snow-covered fields were studded with split-rail fences.

The land reminded him of his mother's property, and Hank was acutely aware that he was just a few hours' drive from his family's home in the Adirondacks. He imagined his mom and siblings sitting around the big dining table with glasses of wine, and promised himself he would do everything in his power to make the ceremony tomorrow.

Everything except walk away from a case.

The door opened behind him and Hank turned to see the face he hadn't even realized he'd been missing. It was there in the hitch of his breath as he looked at her.

"Thanks for coming, Mr. Jared."

Her blonde hair was tied up and away from her face, her eyes calm and clearly grateful.

"Of course."

Was this the face of a traitor?

If Julie Trueblood had hacked into the Navy computers to protect her father, she no doubt believed that what she had done was right. As she held the door wide for him to enter, he realized that the moment might come when he would need to arrest her. Hank crossed the threshold and hoped he wouldn't have to do that.

"The power's been out since this morning," she said. "There's a generator in the barn, but we haven't been able to get it working."

"Maybe I can fix it."

"I'll pretend I wasn't hoping you would say that."

"Why?"

"So I can seem like a tough, independent woman who doesn't need a man to do anything mechanical."

"And fry it up in a pan?"

"Exactly." She had a beautiful smile, he noted, just as it fell. "Of course, I'm already hamming up the damsel in distress routine pretty well."

"I'm glad you called. Someone breaking into your home is unsettling for anyone. Given the circumstances, you were right to call me."

She accepted his words with a nod. "Come on in," she said, stepping aside and motioning for Hank to follow her down the dim hallway. "Watch yourself, it got dark all of a sudden." She trailed her hand along the wall to navigate in the dim light as she called out, "I think it's about time to pull out the candles, Gwen."

They stepped into the kitchen, where a tall woman with flowing blonde curls was busy unpacking boxes of candles and candle holders. "One step ahead of you," she said. She smiled warmly at Hank, and he knew they must often be mistaken for sisters.

"Gwen Trueblood, this is Hank Jared," said Julie.

Hank extended his hand. "That's a lot of firepower, Ms. Trueblood."

"Call me Gwen," she said, lighting candles as she spoke. "I heard you may be able to fix our generator."

"I can give it a try."

"Wonderful," she said, taking a flashlight off the counter and handing it to Hank. "Any tools you might need are out in the barn with the generator. Julie, will you show him where it is?"

"Sure thing." Julie grabbed a down jacket off the back of a kitchen chair and pulled on tall winter boots before leading the way out the back door. When they were alone, she turned and waited for Hank to walk beside her.

"Mr. Jared, I owe you an apology."

He could smell her scent, clean and light, floating on the crisp winter air as he stepped closer. *In a different time and place...*

"It's Hank," he said. "An apology for what?"

"For losing it when you were in my office," she said, her embarrassment plain. "For throwing you out on your ear when you tried to be compassionate."

At her words, Hank remembered the way she had fit in his arms, warm and solid. He knew that he wanted her back there again, and the knowledge made him uneasy. "It must have been quite a shock," he said with sincere sympathy.

Julie frowned. "You know, then."

He nodded. "I did have to work for it, if it makes you feel any better."

She turned back toward the barn and began walking slowly through the snow as she spoke. "I hadn't seen my father in ten years."

Hank knew the admiral wouldn't believe her. "That must have been hard for you."

"I understood it. My father came to see me the day he disappeared."

He raised his eyebrows. "I read the official report. It says the last time you saw him was the night before the disappearance."

"I lied. I got home from school and he was waiting for me at the kitchen table."

The sound of their footsteps through the snow and a blowing wind were the only noises between them. They crossed the last of the field between the house and the barn. Julie lifted the cold metal latch and opened the door, lighting her flashlight for the darkness within.

She led the way as Hank followed closely behind her. At the far end of the barn, she opened a small door and revealed an organized workshop. A red generator had been pulled into the middle of the floor.

"Here it is."

Hank crouched down in front of the machine and extended his hand for the flashlight. She gave it to him and watched as he oriented himself to the older generator.

"The fuel lines are intact. Electrical looks good so far."

"Yeah. I couldn't get a response from the starter."

She did say she had already tried to fix it. He would do well not to underestimate this one. He moved on to examine the starter. "What did you and your dad talk about that day?" he asked.

Julie leaned back against the wall. "He told me what was coming," she said quietly. "The accusations. The charges of treason." Julie took a trembling breath. "He told me he was leaving."

The picture of Julie surrounded by reporters flashed in his mind and Hank felt a surge of adrenaline, as if her father were here and he could beat some sense into the man who was willing to abandon his daughter to save his own skin. *Didn't he know what that would do to her?*

"He told me who set him up."

Hank looked at her in surprise. Nowhere in the file was there mention of any kind of conspiracy.

A part of him clutched at the idea, wishing there was a way for this woman to be clean of her father's sins, but the experienced investigator knew better. McDowell was a father who didn't want his daughter to believe he'd done something terrible.

"His commanding officer gave him messages to decode, just like always. He told him they were from Uzkapostan, but in reality they were coded messages from our own Navy. The content of the messages were things like coordinates and location names, dates, that sort of thing. Nothing that let my father know they were really our own intel."

Julie stared into the distance. "Until the Dermody went down. My father realized that the coordinates of the ship when it was sunk were identical to the coordinates he had decoded the day before."

"What did he do?"

"He escaped." Her features were oddly blank as she continued. "He went to the bank and emptied his accounts, then he came home to talk to me. He told me he would call Barstow and confront him once he was safe…"

"Barstow?"

"Yes, Captain Thomas Barstow. Do you know him? He was my father's commanding officer."

If Hank had been standing, he might have fallen over. He heard himself answer in a monotone voice that sounded like a stranger's. "He's an admiral now."

"An *admiral?*" Her hands were clenched at her sides. "That man should be the one laying in the morgue right now. Not my father. Barstow is the traitor."

Hank watched her fury, saw her chest rise and fall. Hank was a man who trusted his own gut, and his instincts were telling him that Julie Trueblood was telling him the God's honest truth.

"Why did he run?" he asked. "Why not defend himself?"

"My father was born in Uzkapostan. He still has family there."

People had been convicted of espionage on less.

If Julie was correct and the admiral was responsible, it would have been damn near impossible to prove it. Hank turned back to the generator. He needed to think.

"Do you believe me?" she asked.

Hank's hands stilled, but he didn't answer, unsure of what to say. He would have been a lot more comfortable if she hadn't asked the question. His hand fiddled with the starter, and he saw her turn and walk out of the workshop from the corner of his eye. He looked up, staring after her and rubbing his lip with the back of his hand.

Then he was there, grabbing her hand and turning her around to face him, his body too close to hers. He had only meant to stop her. "I believe you," he said.

He could see the desire in her eyes, feel it in the air between them as her scent met his nostrils and he fought for control. He forced his hands to unclench, and released her.

As he stepped back, Julie made the smallest noise deep in her throat, a hum of disappointment. It was enough. He grabbed her, pinning her between his body and the barn as he kissed her forbidden lips with his own.

Lust was there, swift and hot, surprising him with its intensity. She returned his bruising kisses, her passion matching his as they climbed higher, each short of breath, pulses racing.

A loud banging noise startled them apart.

"What was that?" asked Hank.

"It sounded like the barn door slamming in the wind," she said. "But I thought I latched it behind us."

"You did. I saw you."

Hank quickly grabbed the flashlight and pulled out his weapon. "Stay behind me." Halfway back to the door they had come in, they heard the same slamming sound in the opposite direction.

"It's the back door," said Julie. "Not the one we came in." The pair doubled back and walked around a stack of hay, suddenly greeted by an unexpected expanse of white. The open barn door moved slowly in the icy breeze, the snow-covered field beyond glittering in the moonlight as the wind howled ominously.

Clearly visible in the radiant snow was a trail of footprints, leading from the back door of the barn through the field for as far as the eye could see. Julie sank into a squat and bent her head between her knees.

Hank moved closer to the tracks and examined them in the light of his flashlight. "They're recent, but they have about two inches of snow cover," he said, considering. "What time did it stop snowing?"

Julie's gaze dropped lower. "It had already stopped when I got the mail. Noon. Lunchtime."

"So these were made this morning."

"The snow cover might be from blowing snow. It's windy."

"The snow's too wet. Feel it."

Julie didn't move from her crouch.

Hank knelt down next to her. "You okay?"

"Yeah."

"You don't know who made them?"

Julie licked her lips, swallowed. She shook her head. "Gwen and I are the only ones here."

Hank's mind raced, trying to make sense of the tracks. He stared off in the distance and saw another farmhouse, its windows lighted a warm gold in the evening darkness.

And he knew what the intruder had done.

"What time did your power go out?" he asked.

"Ten thirty." Julie's eyes followed his. "They got the generator, too. Didn't they?"

"I think so." Hank extended his hand. "Probably put something in the fuel. I could check but that would take time. We need to get out of here, Julie."

She took the help he offered as she nodded. "I know," she said, rising. "We're taking Gwen with us."

"I know."

"And she'll bring the damn dogs."

"That's okay."

They retraced their steps back to the farmhouse, the wind biting at their hands and faces as they went. Her hand was nestled in the solid warmth of Hank's, something he didn't examine too closely.

"Hank?"

"Yeah?"

"I want to decode that message."

"I know. It's in my car. You can do it on the way."

"Where are we going?"

"To a wedding."

IT TOOK JULIE and Gwen less than twenty minutes to gather what they needed and climb into Hank's SUV. The dogs sat in the backseat with Gwen while Julie took the front, buckling her seat belt with a measure of relief. The irony that she should find comfort in the presence of a Navy officer was not lost on her, and she made a mental note not to trust this man completely.

The car smelled like Hank, and Julie inhaled his scent deep into her lungs. She might not trust him, but he smelled like a million bucks. If someone bottled that smell, they could control the entire female population.

"I had a feeling I wasn't going to need those candles," said Gwen.

The gate of the SUV slammed shut and Hank walked around to the driver's side. Opening the door, he slid across the leather seat and handed Julie a yellow lined paper. "The message from the safe deposit box," he said, reaching to buckle his seat belt.

Julie swallowed against a lump that suddenly formed in her throat. Gingerly she unfolded the single crease and gazed upon her father's handwriting. She had gotten a glimpse of the cipher in her office, but now she had time to really look at what she held in her hands.

Recognition hit her like a blow as she touched the familiar letter shapes with her fingers. Her memory of her father had grown diluted in his absence, misshapen by the accusations that had led to his departure. Sometimes she didn't know who he was anymore, or who he had ever been. The simple paper in her hand was like a snapshot of her real dad, sweet and strong.

Gone forever.

Her eyes burned.

"You recognize the handwriting," said Hank.

Julie reached into the bag between her feet. "Yes," she said quietly. She pulled out a spiral notebook and a pencil, never looking in Hank's direction.

"It was like that with my David," said Gwen thoughtfully. "The littlest thing, out of the blue, like a light in the darkness. Then I'd feel the pain all over again when I realized he was gone."

Hank's eyes in the rearview mirror were sympathetic. "Who was David?" he asked.

"My husband," she said, smiling fondly. "It will be eleven years ago in January that he was killed in a skiing accident."

"I'm sorry."

"Me, too." Gwen sat up a little straighter. "Julie, Julie. Do you still remember how to crack those codes?"

"It's been a long time," she said. "I don't know if it will come back to me."

"That message is meant for you, Julie. Your daddy didn't write that for anyone else. I'm sure you'll know just what to do."

Julie wished she had Gwen's confidence in her abilities. Opening to a clean page in the notebook, she began writing.

"Can I ask what you're doing?" said Hank.

"Counting letter frequencies."

Hank cursed softly under his breath. "I forgot about Chip." He pulled out his cell phone.

"Who's Chip?" asked Julie.

"My buddy at the NSA. I asked him to run that through the computer."

Julie's wasn't happy he had brought in a professional cryptographer. She was reminded once again that she and Hank had different objectives. "It won't do any good."

"So he told me." Hank opened his cell phone and dialed. He left a message on Chip's voicemail to call him back ASAP. "His wife is eight months pregnant with twins. Maybe she went into labor."

Julie worked quietly as they drove, completing the frequency chart and looking for letter patterns. It was very basic work, but she had to start somewhere.

"Julie, I'm sorry to interrupt you," said Hank.

"What is it?"

"I need to call my mother and tell her we're on our way. I will tell her and my sister the truth, but I think it would be an easier visit if we have a cover story for everyone else."

That sounded reasonable. "Okay."

"So, I was thinking you could be my date for the wedding, and Gwen could be your aunt from Vermont who just happens to know my sister. Maybe that's how we met—through your aunt and my sister."

"I do some jewelry design," piped Gwen from the backseat., "including wedding bands."

"Perfect," said Hank. "Actually, last I heard the wedding bands were MIA, so that might actually be true before we're done here."

"What a coincidence!" said Gwen, smiling from ear to ear. "It's like serendipity. Don't you just love when the universe aligns to make things happen?"

Julie turned around in her seat to glare at her aunt like she was insane. Gwen rewarded her effort with a wide grin, and Julie shook her head. To Hank, she asked, "You want me to be your date for your sister's wedding?"

"It seems like the easiest way to explain a stranger's presence at a wedding, don't you think?"

"Yes, I guess it is." She turned back to her notebook. "Just don't expect me to do the chicken dance at the reception."

"We're more of an electric slide kind of family."

Julie stared at him blankly. "I really need to do this," she said, holding up the notebook.

"Of course. Sorry." A moment later, he slid his shoulders to the left in a wave-like motion.

"Boogie woogie woogie," came Gwen's high-pitched voice, earning her an appreciative chuckle from Hank.

"Really, Gwen?" said Julie.

"Oh, pooh, Julie. Fine, I'll be quiet."

The three of them cruised the rest of the way into the Adirondacks and New York State without another word.

IT WAS JUST after nine o'clock, but it felt much later to Hank as he drove along the winding roads that snaked up the side of Moon Lake Mountain. He kept careful watch for deer and other wild animals, everyday hazards for those driving through the heavily wooded area. Tall pines flanked the road on either side, with the occasional mailbox denoting a home nestled somewhere behind the dense trees.

His mother had been so happy when he phoned to tell her he was coming after all, and he was just as excited as she was.

Beside him, Julie worked diligently in the dim light of the overhead reading lamp. Gwen had fallen asleep shortly after they stopped for coffee at a diner called the Truck Stop Inn, and Hank could hear faint snoring, though he wasn't sure if it came from the woman or one of the dogs.

"I can't stare at this anymore," said Julie, closing the notebook and returning it to her bag on the floor. She took a long sip of cold coffee.

Hank shook his shoulders and grimaced. "I don't know how you do that."

"The code breaking?"

"Cold coffee. Gives me the heebie-jeebies."

"Tough guy like you, bothered by a little cold coffee?" She smiled at him, her voice playful.

"It's like kryptonite to Superman."

"Did you really just call yourself Superman?"

Hank gave her his best offended look. "Not exactly. But I could be Superman."

"Really."

"Absolutely."

"I don't think so, hot shot Navy man."

"Whoa, wait a minute. The similarities are downright eerie if you give me a chance."

Julie laughed dismissively. "Well, there's the cold coffee thing. I'd love to hear the other similarities."

"Superman's tall. I'm tall."

"One."

"Superman has dark hair."

"This car ride just got a lot longer."

"Superman loved his family, fought for right over

wrong, and would do anything for Lois Lane." He held up his fingers as he counted off his reasons.

"Ah, Lois. I was wondering about her. Why isn't she your date for the wedding? Important assignment from the paper?"

"You were wondering if I had a girlfriend?" he asked, looking at her intensely, the slightest smile playing on the corners of his lips.

She looked like she swallowed a bug. "Not really. I was just playing along."

"Playing along," he agreed, nodding. "I see." She was full of it, and the knowledge pleased him immensely. "There is no Lois. But someday when I find her, I will do anything for that woman."

The smallest voice in the back of his head suggested he already had, which was ridiculous.

"How much farther to your mom's house?"

"We're almost there now."

A wide right turn ended in one final hill as the SUV crested the highest point of the mountain. A wide vista opened before them, the light of the full moon clearly visible without the cover of the forest, Moon Lake glistening in the rays of its namesake.

"Beautiful," she said softly.

Hank had been watching her, and silently agreed, but he was thinking nothing of the landscape and everything about the woman beside him.

"The house is up here another mile or two."

"Great," she said, rubbing her hands on her thighs. "Who's going to be there?"

"My mom, Marianne. Tough as nails, with a soft side. You'll like her." *If she likes you,* he added to himself. His mother was not one to suffer fools gladly, but Hank wasn't overly concerned. If anything, his mother would probably like Julie too much. That's why he made sure to tell her that Julie was only pretending to be his girlfriend. "She took over the family business when my dad passed away a few years ago."

"I'm sorry."

"Thank you."

"What's the family business?"

"Our first product was organic fruit soap. We've expanded over the years to include natural gardening products."

"Wait, as in Uncle Billy's Rockin' Organic Fruit Soap?"

"That's the one."

Julie laughed. "Who came up with that name?"

"Kelly. My father thought it would be a fun family project to market it at the local Agway one summer. I designed the packaging, Norah wrote the copy. We never expected it to take off."

"Who's Norah?"

"My older sister. She'll be there tonight, along with her husband Steve. She's a professional cellist with the Boston Philharmonic; he teaches linguistics at Northeastern."

"Any more brothers or sisters?"

"Nope. That's the whole family."

Julie rubbed her hands together. "Your mom is Marianne, Kelly's marrying Ron, and Norah's married to Steve."

"Relax. You'll be fine."

"I'm not good with names. I make associations to remember them."

"What do you mean?"

"I get pictures in my head that help me remember. Like your sister, Kelly. Kelly Ogden was my best friend in the fourth grade. So I picture her standing at the altar with Ronald McDonald."

Hank knew that the polished and athletic Ron wouldn't appreciate this game at all. "Go on."

"For your sister, I picture Nora Roberts playing the cello on the back of one of her books."

"Who's Nora Roberts?"

Julie looked at him like he had blasphemed. "Just one of the best romance novel authors of all time, thank you very much."

Hank raised his hands in mock surrender. "What about Steve?"

"The book with the cello is about a linguistics professor at Northeastern who falls for an older student. A music major. It's very touching."

"Is that a real book?"

"Of course not. Didn't you hear me? I'm just trying

to remember their names."

He laughed at her absurd thought process. "Whatever works for you." He slowed down as they drove alongside several hundred feet of stacked stone fence, then turned onto a driveway that meandered away from the road and back toward the lake. "This is it."

Julie turned around and woke up Gwen, then watched as the tree-lined driveway opened to a wide, snow-covered lawn. The big house was a mixture of Tudor and log cabin styles, clearly one-of-a-kind in its design. There was a three-car detached garage and what looked to be a large screened porch off the side of the residence.

Hank pulled to a stop in the circular driveway. "Leave the bags. I'll come out for them in a bit." Julie opened her door and stepped out into the chilly night air.

The front door opened and a slender woman with long gray and black hair appeared under the porch light, some fifteen feet from the car.

Hank helped Julie with her bag as Gwen stepped out and stretched her legs. Raising his voice, he said, "Mom, I'd like you to meet Julie and Gwen Trueblood. Ladies, this is my mom."

Julie swore quietly.

Hank realized her problem at once. He sang quietly, "Sit right back and you'll hear a tale, a tale of a mighty ship…"

4

"AND THIS IS where you and Julie will be staying," said Marianne, opening the door to a single bedroom with a queen size bed and its own bathroom. Julie's cheeks heated as she thought about sharing that bed with Hank.

Hank spoke in a low voice. "Ma, I told you it's not like that."

"I understand that, dear. But this is Kelly's wedding weekend and we have a full house. I had to do some rearranging to get you a room at all. Gwen has to sleep in the office with cousin Josie on the last air mattress. This," she said, gesturing to the red and gold guest room, "is the best I can do. There are clean towels in the bathroom closet and an extra blanket in the chest," she said firmly, walking away.

"I'm sorry," Hank said to Julie. "I'll sleep on the floor."

"Damn straight, you will."

"Come on. I'll introduce you around."

Julie looked around the room, wishing she could barricade herself within it. "Do you have to?"

He looked at her quizzically. "What's wrong?"

"What if someone asks how we met, or something else I don't have an answer for?"

"Lie."

"I'm a terrible liar."

"Well, then, this should be good practice for you." He steered her toward the stairs, almost running into his sister.

"There you are. Ron and I would like to say a few words before everyone heads out," she said, gesturing downstairs. The rehearsal dinner ended shortly before Hank and Julie arrived, and close members of the family were still congregated at the house.

Julie begrudgingly followed Hank down the stairs, and took her place next to him in the entranceway between the foyer and living room.

Kelly and Ron made a striking couple. She was petite, with the same honeyed skin as her brother and dark hair that fell in lustrous waves down her back. Ron was much taller and quite muscular, like a model or fitness trainer. His head was completely bald and shiny, his kind and handsome face suggesting he might have been a blonde or a redhead at one time.

"We want each of you to know what it means to us

that you're here to share in our wedding. I wasn't sure this day would ever come," she said, garnering a laugh from those who knew the couple well, "and well, we just wanted to say thank you."

"Mom," she continued, "we owe you a special thanks." To the room, she said, "When the caterer double-booked and cancelled on us last week, my mother stepped up and offered to do the cooking herself." Gasps could be heard around the room. "We couldn't do this without you, Mom." Claps and a few cheers followed.

"And to my brother, Hank, who will be walking me down the aisle tomorrow," she paused and bit her lip to keep the tears that threatened in check, "I am so very glad you were able to make it. There's only one person I'd rather have at my side, and I'm sure he is smiling down from heaven at the thought that you will stand in his place."

Ron put his arm around his fiancé and raised his glass in Hank's direction. Julie felt a knot in her throat at the sense of loss these people so obviously shared, on the eve of such celebration. It occurred to her that Hank had missed the rehearsal dinner because he was helping her at the farmhouse. Would he have missed the entire wedding if she had still needed him in Vermont?

Lois Lane was one lucky woman.

Hank looked up at that moment. Their gazes met

and locked, sharing a moment of intimate appraisal. Everything about this man attracted her, and she felt a tingling sensation in her abdomen. Hank's eyes dropped to her lips, and she knew he wanted to kiss her.

She flashed back to the barn, and their brief, fiery kisses, her cheeks heating at the memory. The realization that she wanted him even more now set her into a small panic.

Forget about Superman. He isn't even trustworthy.

She broke eye contact and took a step away.

Kelly and Ron finished their remarks, and Julie turned on her heel and walked away from Hank. She'd rather face a hundred and one people who thought she was in love with him than face the man himself.

She spent forty-five minutes in the kitchen, listening to his great aunt Phoebe describe her trip to Paris, then ten more talking to Ron, who got her a beer. Feeling pleasantly relaxed from the drink, she slipped up the stairs to turn in for the night.

Hank caught up to her just outside the bedroom door, turning her around by touching her shoulder.

"Do you know that everyone in that room thinks we're fighting?"

Julie bristled at his tone.

"I may be sleeping on the floor," he continued, "but there's no need for the whole world to know it."

"Don't be ridiculous. I was only kidding. You can

sleep with me."

"What?" His pupils dilated and he leaned toward her.

"In fact," she said, looking up at him through her lashes, "I'm kind of tired."

"Hey, Hank," said a voice just behind him. He turned and saw Kelly's fiancé. "I'm going to get heading home. I'm glad you were able to make it," said Ron as he shook Hank's hand. "It means a lot to Kelly, and to me."

"Couldn't have kept me away if you'd tried," he said, smiling at the other man. "Ron, did you meet my girlfriend, Julie?"

"Yes, downstairs," said Ron.

Julie smirked, leaning on the door jam. "Ron was telling me how he and Kelly met."

"Now, don't go telling on me before the ceremony. I've almost made it without being discovered." Ron chuckled, a goofy grin on his face. "I'm going to head home. I'll see you both at the church tomorrow. Sorry if I interrupted anything," he said with a wink, then walked away.

Hank rounded on Julie. "He did interrupt something, didn't he?"

Julie's eyes went wide. She made certain Ron was out of earshot before she whispered, "I was just pretending."

He moved into her personal space, his eyes smoldering and purposeful.

She took a step backward into the bedroom and watched as he advanced on her by equal measure, closing the door quietly behind him.

"Were you pretending in the barn?"

"The barn?" she asked, continuing her backward retreat. She stopped when the back of her legs hit the bed.

The bed!

Her lungs sucked in air as her pulse hammered away.

"You do remember the barn. I can see it all over your face." he bent his head purposefully, his hand reaching for the back of her neck.

Julie wanted it so badly. She wanted this strong, sexy man to kiss her like mad, to take possession of her body and make her forget everything else, but a nagging voice wailed in her head. Her life was a complete disaster. She just lost her father. She was being hunted by a crazy ex-boyfriend or her father's killer, maybe both. You don't find love in the middle of all that.

You find men who prey on women who don't have their shit together.

The thought had her pushing him away. "Whoa, hold on a minute. I was just putting on a show for your new brother-in-law," she said, standing taller and squaring her shoulders.

"He's not my brother-in-law until tomorrow," He corrected her, staring at her full breasts, then back to her lips.

"I'm going to take a shower," she said, sidestepping to get past Hank's wide shoulders. Walking to the dresser, she began digging in her overnight bag for her pajamas, flustered when she couldn't find what she wanted. Feeling like an idiot, she picked up the whole bag, went in the bathroom, and locked the door.

She sank down onto the toilet seat, clutching her bag, and breathed deeply as she closed her eyes. Sadness and fatigue surrounded her in a drenching wave. She was enjoying the sexual banter with Hank, then suddenly she saw herself as he must see her—a grieving, messed up woman with nowhere to go and just a handful of people who loved her.

Hank wasn't interested in her awesome personality. He was a Navy officer who just happened to be sharing her bedroom tonight, and figured he may as well get lucky. Kill two birds with one stone. She knew his type well and had little respect for them. The familiar uniform just added insult to injury, pointing out what she should never have forgotten.

Hank Jared was not someone she could trust.

Julie stood and turned the hot water on full force as she began to undress. She resented the fact that she was stuck here, pretending to be someone she wasn't just to stay one step ahead of a nameless, faceless enemy. As the water sluiced over her skin, she shivered in spite of the heat. Her mind was full of images—a burned out hotel room, the window seat at Gwen's house, a rusty red generator and footprints in the snow.

She thought of the message from the safe deposit box as she let the water run down her bent head and shoulders. Her quick cryptanalysis in the car had begun to awaken memories of processes long since forgotten. She knew and understood every class of cipher ever popularized, from simple substitution and Masonics to the latest in computer generated random keys and transport layer security. Her mind played the options like notes on a score, trying different combinations and looking for patterns that would confirm or deny their collusion.

Grabbing a bar of sweet-smelling soap, she began to wash away the experience of the day while her mind raced through secret codes and memories. Something was bothering her about the message, interfering with her thoughts like a car parked in the middle of a freeway. There was a familiarity about the cipher that eluded her, ringing the faintest of bells in her jangled memory.

Frustrated with herself, she tried to stop focusing on it, hoping it would gather itself together in her subconscious and emerge as a coherent whole if she left it alone.

Julie turned off the water and opened the shower

curtain, gazing through the steam at the bathroom door with annoyance. It was going to be a long night with Hank sleeping on the floor just feet from her bed. The thought of him in such close proximity made her pulse pick up, and she cursed her own attraction to the man.

She dried her hair with the towel before wrapping it around her torso. The pajamas she'd frantically been searching for earlier were now clearly visible at the top of her duffle bag.

That figures.

An old favorite, they were knit of soft green cotton, with a boxy tee and wide pants that were about as alluring as a potato sack.

"Thank God for ugly pajamas," she said to herself.

The bedroom was dark when she emerged, with just a small nightlight in the bathroom behind her to light the way. Maybe he was already asleep. She stood still, waiting for her eyes to adjust to the inky blackness.

"I'm on the floor, between the bathroom and the bed. Don't step on me."

She could just make out the bed posts and began walking toward them in the darkness. Three steps in, she kicked something solid.

"Ouch!"

"Sorry!"

"Seriously? Because I didn't tell you exactly where I was?"

"I said I'm sorry."

"Well then, I guess it didn't hurt."

"Oh please, you're fine."

"You just kicked me."

"What are you, a baby? Because you're carrying on like one."

She heard him stand up in front of her. "You're calling me names, now?"

"If the shoe fits…" she was startled when he pulled her against him.

"Shut up, Julie," he said, kissing her roughly. She pushed against him half-heartedly, even as her mouth responded to his and kissed him back passionately. His hand slipped beneath her top to caress the bare skin of her back.

HE HADN'T MEANT to kiss her.

She had been playing games with him, flirting and retreating, and Hank didn't like games. While she was in the bathroom, he made the decision to keep their relationship professional. He had no intention of jeopardizing his career for Julie Trueblood.

That was, until she opened the bathroom door and he saw her body silhouetted in the light of the doorway, the thin fabric of her pajamas teasing him like the sexiest lingerie.

His body's response had been instantaneous.

This woman made him feel like he was in high school, all hormones and raging lust. He might die if he couldn't get close to her, couldn't rub her smooth skin and feel her body pressed against him.

Her breasts pushed at his bare chest, separated from him only by the light material, and his hand reach up in an intimate caress, making her moan. Her head fell back and he grabbed the hem of her shirt, lifting it upward.

Julie jumped back, recoiling from his hands. "I don't want to do this."

Hank's stare bored into her own in the dark room. "Liar," he said thickly. "You want to as much as I do."

Her chin lifted in denial and she opened her mouth to speak.

He didn't want to hear it. He was tired, he was aggravated, and he was bordering on crazy. He sank down on his makeshift bed before she could pretend she wasn't on fire, just like he was. "Goodnight, Julie."

She stood shock still for a moment before finishing her walk to the high poster bed, and scurried under the covers. "Goodnight."

The carpeted floor was rigid beneath Hank's frustrated form, and he punched the pillow in an attempt to get comfortable. He imagined resting his head on Julie's soft breasts instead, and knew that sleep would be hard to come by this evening.

"Just so you know, tomorrow's a big deal to me and

my family. I'd appreciate it if you try to be a convincing girlfriend."

"What does that mean, exactly?"

"Pretend you like me, Julie. Don't cross your arms over your chest or walk away when I speak to you. Smile at me once in a while. Dance with me at the reception and hold my hand if you can stand the thought."

He was about to ask if she'd heard him, when she finally replied, "Okay."

"Okay, what?"

"I'll pretend to like you."

"Great. Thank you. I hope the experience isn't too painful for you."

"Goodnight, Hank."

"Goodnight, Julie."

THE PUNGENT SMELL of wood smoke burned Julie's nostrils and woke her from a sound sleep. She sat up in bed to a room she didn't recognize, completely alone and terrified. Reaching for the bedside lamp, she turned the switch and heard a click, but no light came on.

In the distance, someone laughed maniacally, and an old red generator appeared next to the bed, lit as if by a spotlight. Her father stood before her, his lifeless eyes staring at a fixed point on the wall. In his hands, he held a severed electrical cord. "Did you check the starter?" he asked.

Julie heard a piercing scream, but did not realize it was her own.

The bedroom door opened, and she could see leaping flames of orange and red violently consuming the hallway beyond. Gwen appeared through the wall of fire completely unscathed, and entered the room wearing an old-fashioned nurse's uniform.

"Telegram," said Gwen. "I have a telegram here for Julie McDowell."

"That's me," Julie said, but her aunt didn't seem to hear her. "That's me," she said again, but to no avail.

Next to the bed, the generator roared to life with a great shudder, and Julie pressed her hand to her frantically beating heart. She felt rich beading beneath her fingers and looked down at the bodice of a white wedding gown.

Hank!

She had to save Hank! She knew he was in this house, burning in the fire that had been meant for her alone. Desperate to find him, she threw back the covers on the bed and got up, standing face-to-face with a burned-out skeleton in a Navy officer's uniform.

The screaming wouldn't stop this time. Flames broke through the door to the bedroom. Nurse Gwen stood next to an eye chart emblazoned with the beginning of the cipher from the safe deposit box.

"Cover your left eye, please. What does this say?" she asked Julie.

"I don't know! I don't know!" she wailed. The dead body in the Navy uniform grabbed at her arms, shaking her. "Get off of me! Let me go!" she wailed in horror.

"Julie!" Shouted the corpse. "Julie! Wake up! It's just a dream!"

"Get off of me! I have to find Hank!" she screamed, yanking her arms free of her captor and connecting with the solid bones of his face.

"Julie! It's me! It's Hank! Wake up!"

Hank was here? Confusion had her fiery dream evaporating into nothingness. Slowly the weight of her eyelids lifted and she saw Hank's face just inches from her own in the darkness.

Her hysterical screaming stopped, and a relief-stricken wail began. He was okay. He was safe from the fire. "You're all right," she said between great gasps of air.

He wrapped her into his arms, pulling her tightly against his chest as he spoke in a calming voice. "I'm fine. You were having a bad dream. Everything's okay now." He cuddled her against his warm body, gently stroking her hair.

"Everything was on fire. My father was there, and he was..." she tried to find the words to describe her gruesome vision, "burned. It was horrible."

Julie wiped her eyes, her hands shaking.

"How awful for you."

She realized that Hank had actually seen her father after the fire, and cringed at the thought. She didn't want to imagine what he had seen, didn't want to know he had seen it.

"There was a generator with a severed cord. And Gwen was there in a nurse's uniform, trying to give me a telegram."

"It sounds like your mind has had a lot to take in over the last couple of days."

"Yes." She snuggled closer to his chest, burying her face in his T-shirt.

"Was I in your dream?" he asked, his fingers tentatively stroking her shoulder. "You called my name."

"Yes," she said, suddenly shy. "I couldn't see you, but I knew you were in the building and the fire was going to get you. I was trying to save you." She left out the part about the wedding gown.

Hank gently rubbed her back and she felt her body slowly relax into the mattress. "Hank?"

"Mmm hmm?"

"Are we safe here?"

"Of course."

"Are you sure they don't know where we are?"

"I'm positive. No one followed us here, and I didn't tell anyone where we went." He hadn't even told Barstow, a fact which might come back to haunt him.

"How else would someone know where we are?"

"I don't know."

Hank's brow furrowed as Julie settled back into the crook of his arm and fell back asleep.

IF JULIE WAS correct, then not only were she and Gwen in danger, but his entire family. Hank gave himself a mental shake. Her bad feeling could not be based in fact.

They hadn't been followed, of that he was certain. He had deliberately set the GPS to avoid expressways so he could better watch the cars around them. Still, his gut didn't like this. The people who Hank loved most were gathered in this house. Was it possible he had put them all in danger by bringing Julie and Gwen here?

He laid awake in the night, Julie curled by his side, for some hours after that. His eyes finally succumbed to sleep as the first light of Christmas Eve beckoned on the horizon.

JULIE WAS GONE when Hank woke up to rays of bright sunshine on his face. He'd have to remember to close the blinds tonight.

He caught a whiff of coffee on the air, his mind turning to the day ahead. There must be a million things to do, and they had let him sleep late. He pulled a green polo over his head and went to see what he could do to help.

Voices flowed up the stairway, the sound reminiscent of a million other family get-togethers. For a moment, he imagined his father downstairs with the others, talking and laughing over morning coffee. Hank's feet stilled on the top step, his eyes landing on the familiar photograph of him with his dad, fishing poles in their hands.

For just a moment, he was sure he could feel his father's comforting presence, smell the scent that belonged to him alone.

I love you, Dad.

Hank walked down the steps, smiling, suddenly certain his father would not miss Kelly's wedding after all.

"Well, look who finally decided to get out of bed," said Marianne. She was standing at the sink filling a large coffee urn with water, her warm smile contrasting her reproachful tone. "We were going to sneak in and take turns poking you with a stick in another half an hour."

"You should have woken me."

Gwen, Kelly and Julie sat at the table, working on something small with their hands. Julie stood up, flashing Hank a bright smile. "Merry Christmas Eve, sweetie," she said, leaning in for a quick peck on the lips. Hank's jaw dropped open. "Want some coffee?"

"That'd be great."

She walked to the counter and poured coffee from a Thermos. Hank watched as she put in one scoop of sugar and a small splash of milk. Someone had been paying attention when they stopped for coffee yesterday.

"Thanks," he said, taking the cup from her. He could get used to this.

"Gwen's making wedding bands for the ceremony today," said Julie.

"Just temporaries," said Gwen. "I don't think the bride and groom want to wear jewelry made out of paperclips forever."

"They're so beautiful, we just might," said Kelly. "Look, Hank."

She walked to him, holding something out for him to see. It was an intricate weaving of silver metal, strung with what appeared to be shining blue gemstones and glittering diamonds.

"That's incredible. You made that out of paperclips? What did you use for stones?"

"The colored ones are beads from Gwen's necklace, and the diamond-like ones are tiny crystals."

Hank eyed Gwen incredulously. "You just happened to have those things with you?"

"It was the strangest thing," said Gwen. "I was packing for our adventure and I stopped short as I was about to head downstairs. I forgot my beaded blue topaz necklace, I thought to myself. I hadn't intended to bring it, mind you. But after years of these kinds of thoughts you know when to listen."

She threaded a tiny blue bead onto a thick wire. "So I grabbed the necklace out of my jewelry box and asked the universe," she said dramatically, raising her head up high, "Is there anything else I need to bring? Then I thought about those crystals in my studio. So I grabbed those, too."

A chill ran up Hank's spine.

"Does that happen to you a lot?" asked Kelly, sitting back down.

Gwen touched the younger woman's hand on the table. "It does."

Next to Hank, Julie stepped on her tip toes and whispered in his ear. "Can opener." At his quizzical look, she nodded in Gwen's direction.

"The first time it ever happened, I was in college," said Gwen. "I was leaving my dorm room to go to class when I thought, 'Oh, I've forgotten my can opener.' I didn't need a can opener for class, of course." She took a sip of her coffee. "That day at lunch, a friend pulled out a can of soup, but had forgotten to bring a can opener. I said, 'That would explain why I brought this.'"

"That's amazing," said Kelly.

"It is. Very helpful, too," she said with a wink.

Hank turned thoughtful eyes to Julie, remembering

her concerns for their safety here at the house. "Does that ever happen to you?"

"Never."

"I'm afraid the universe lacks a large enough sledge hammer with which to hit my niece over the head," said Gwen.

"What's that supposed to mean?" asked Julie.

"It means you know more than you are willing to admit, even to yourself."

She cocked her head to the side. "Maybe. Maybe not."

Turning to Hank, she smiled and slipped her arm around his waist. "Can I help with anything today?"

He nearly spit coffee all over himself. "I have no idea." Just to see what she would do, he put his arm around her shoulders and pulled her close, dumbfounded when she settled pleasantly at his side. He shook his head. "What needs to be done, Ma?"

"More than you can possibly imagine. I have a list for you," she said, reaching to the bulletin board on the side of the refrigerator and handing him a piece of paper. He was oddly pleased to see his name scrawled across the top of it, just as he imagined it would be. "You're in charge of setting up the big things at the church hall. The tables and chairs, the buffet and the bar. Steve will go with you."

"I can handle that. Are the tables and chairs being delivered or do I need to pick them up?"

"Delivered. They should be there already. You need to go to the liquor store and stock the bar. Mid-shelf, Hank. No cheap stuff, nothing too expensive either." Marianne stirred an enormous pot with a spoon nearly three feet long.

"Julie, how would you feel about doing the decorations? I would head over there myself, but I need to stay here and work on the food."

"I'm almost done with these rings, Marianne. I'd be happy to give you a hand with the cooking," said Gwen.

"That would be wonderful," said Marianne, her shoulders dropping and a sigh escaping as she worked.

"And I," said Julie, "will decorate. What do you have in mind, Kelly?"

"A winter wonderland," she said excitedly. "The centerpieces are done, but not much else. The church hall was supposed to be vacant yesterday so I could get in there take care of it myself, but there was a funeral reception so nothing is finished. I have a lot of materials, but no real plans. There must be hundreds of yards of red ribbon alone."

"What else do you have?"

"Gold spray paint, white snow paint, oodles of fake snow, a few artificial Christmas trees, gold glitter, a whole mess of evergreen garland…"

"Julie," Hank interrupted. "I'm going to wash up so we can head over to the church. About fifteen minutes?" asked Hank.

"Sure. I'll be ready." She flashed him a radiant smile. "What do you have in mind for the head table?"

JULIE PULLED THE door to the SUV closed behind her and reached for her notebook on the middle console. "Isn't Steve coming with us?" she asked.

"He's meeting us there."

She opened to a clean page, intending to work on the cipher, and found her thoughts drifting to her father. An unconscious frown came over her face.

"You okay?"

"This message is beginning to drive me crazy," she said, then decided to tell him the truth. "And I miss my dad. I miss my dad a lot."

He took the key out of the ignition and turned to face her. "I'm missing my dad a lot today, too."

She nodded, feeling tears begin to build up in her eyes. She didn't want to have this conversation with him, but she was wise enough to see that she needed it.

"It's been so busy, coming here. Everything that's going on. I haven't had a chance..."

"To mourn."

She nodded vigorously, an embarrassing sob escaping as she did.

"I just want to crawl under a rock and be alone for a while."

He bowed his head. "I know. I wish I could give you that chance." His lips pressed together in a thin line. "We could pretend you're sick, but I really would feel better if you were with me."

"I'd feel better, too. I'm just babbling."

He reached for her hand and held it. "You're not babbling. And you're entitled to feel however you feel."

She took a deep breath and took her hand back from Hank's, again reaching for the notebook in her lap.

"Chip," he said, digging in his pocket for his cell phone.

"He never called you back?"

"No."

This is Chip Vandermead. I can't take your call right now...

Hank sighed. "Chip, it's Hank. I'm getting worried. Call me when you get this." He hung up the phone and started the engine.

"Do you think she had the babies?"

"I don't know."

"What's the alternative?"

Hank's eyes met hers as he pulled out of the driveway. "I don't know that either. That's what worries me." He turned his windshield wipers on as snow began to collect on the glass. "Tell me something. If Chip can't crack that code, why are you so confident you'll be able to?"

"Gwen says it was meant for me. That my father wrote it, intending for me to be able to read it."

"Chip said that short codes are harder to break."

"As a rule, they are. Often it's impossible. But Gwen's right—if my father wanted me to be able to read this, he would have made sure to use a cipher or symbol I would recognize."

The moment she said the words, Julie froze. In the space of an instant, she understood what her subconscious had been trying to tell her since she first saw the secret message.

"Oh my God. Oh my God! A cipher I would recognize!" she yelled, clutching Hank's arm. "Let me use your phone, please!"

"What is it? What do you recognize?"

Grabbing Hank's phone, she opened the web browser and typed in the first six characters of the cipher from memory. Clever bastard, she thought, smiling at his ingenuity as she used the internet to quickly confirm what she already knew.

"The first line of the cipher isn't part of his message at all. It's the beginning of a message that got King Leopold the Fourth executed for espionage in the Fourteenth Century!" she smacked his upper arm, a big grin lighting her face.

"Your father knew you would realize *that*?"

"He taught me the Leopold cipher when I was little. It was fun for a kid, because you make this decoder out of rings on a dowel. I brought it to show and tell."

"Sounds like a secret decoder ring."

"It is sort of, yes."

"So now you can decode the message."

Julie scoffed. "Not even close. Knowing the type of cipher is half the battle. I still need to break the code."

"Don't you just have to build the rings?"

"It's not that simple. They have to be aligned on an axle in the right order. There are thirteen factorial possible positions, which means millions of possibilities. That's the strength of the cipher."

"What do you do now?"

"I need to find the keyword. It will tell me what order to put the rings onto the axle. It could be a number, or a word or phrase." She was missing the vast capabilities of the computers that surrounded her when she was at work. "If I had access to my computers, I would write a simple program which tries out all possible combinations, then just wait until it hits on one that makes sense."

"How long does that take?"

"Hard to say. It depends on how lucky you are, and how many machines you have searching for the right combination simultaneously. Days, weeks, maybe months. It certainly would be a lot easier if I could figure out the combination on my own, in whatever way my father expected me to discover it." Julie bit down on her lip and looked out the window, unseeing.

Hank pulled into the parking lot of a small white church with a tall four-sided steeple. "This is it." Steve's sedan was already in the parking lot.

"Can I use your phone one more time? I'm going to have Becky use my work computers to search for the key."

"Sure."

When Hank waited for her to make her call, she looked at him uncomfortably. "I'll be right in."

She doesn't want me to hear her conversation.

Clearly she didn't trust him, which reminded him of Admiral Barstow and his own deception. If Julie knew who he worked for, he'd be guilty by association.

And what about her? Hank still wasn't sure if Julie sympathized with her father. She may even have helped him commit espionage, or deleted his Navy records. Was she working to hide important facts right now?

The unpleasant thought stuck with him as he walked to the door of the church and let himself in. The building appeared to be empty, its long wooden pews glistening in the light from the stained glass windows. Hank looked at the simple altar and the cross behind it, and found himself saying a silent prayer.

Please let her be innocent. Please let her trust me.

5

JULIE PUT HER hands on her hips and surveyed her handiwork. The church basement had been greatly improved, but it was a far cry from "transformed".

"These lights have to go," she said.

Raising his head, Hank looked up at the fluorescent fixtures that ran the entire space. "The fluorescents?" he asked, raising his eyebrows high.

"They're horrible, aren't they? I feel like I'm shopping in a discount clothing store, not enjoying a winter wonderland with my one true love."

"Maybe Kelly and Ron are a couple of tree huggers. Maybe they *love* fluorescent lights. Maybe," he said, raising his index finger, "they'd be angry if you changed them."

"Just the other day," said Steve, taking a break from arranging tables, "I heard Kelly talking about how she hoped to be married under LEDs. But if that's not possible, I'm sure fluorescents are the next best thing."

"Marriage is all about compromise," agreed Hank.

Julie rounded on the men. Clearly, they were thick as thieves. "Do you two lunkheads think this is Kelly's dream? To celebrate her marriage to Ron under lights that give everything the horrible glow of energy efficiency?" she shift her weight onto one hip and crossed her arms. "I think not."

Hank rubbed the back of his neck. "What do you suggest?"

"How about candles?"

"Candles to light the whole space?" He spun around, holding his arms out to his sides. "Do you know how many candles that would take?"

"Is there a DJ coming? He might have some lights for the dance floor," said Julie.

"I don't know if there's a DJ, or a band, or the Boys Choir of Harlem."

"Who are you calling?"

"My mother," he said, walking to the far end of the room.

Julie busied herself by decorating the last Christmas tree with red ribbon while she waited.

"There's a DJ, and he comes with his own light display. Including," his eyes lit up, "his very own spinning disco ball."

"Oh, well, you have to have a disco ball to do the Electric Slide."

"Bingo."

"All right. The DJ's lights should illuminate that half of the room fairly well, and the centerpieces each have one candle. We can bump that up to five or six..." her voice trailed off as she surveyed the large basement.

"That's still a hell of a lot of candles," said Hank.

"Sounds like a fire hazard," said Steve.

"Got a better idea?"

Hank snapped his fingers. "As a matter of fact, I do."

Two hours later, Julie finished hanging her last strand of white Christmas lights and stepped back to admire the room. Gone was the drab and depressing basement, and in its place glittered a gorgeous, romantic setting for the beginning of Kelly and Ron's life together. She also added four more candles to each centerpiece, not wanting to give up her idea completely.

Steve had been summoned back to the house to help deliver food to neighbors' ovens and refrigerators, and Julie was feeling his absence. He had acted as a buffer, and she wasn't sure what to do with Hank now that it was just the two of them.

He stood on a step ladder, connecting several strands of the twinkling lights to the center of the ceiling in a spoke-like pattern. Julie watched his beautiful body in silent appreciation, the muscles of his arms and shoulders clearly visible beneath his t-shirt. The gentle light that filled the room flattered him, glorifying his amber skin, and Julie savored the chance to observe him unnoticed.

In a different time and place, she could have cared for this man. She knew it like she knew her own face in the mirror. Julie had been looking for Hank Jared in every man she had ever met, and now she understood why each of them had left her cold and unaffected.

I never knew a man this good could care about me—know every skeleton in my closet and want me anyway.

Hank stepped off the ladder to grab the last string of lights from the floor, climbing again to add it to the bundle. Raising his head, he caught her eye and smiled.

Julie felt her breath hitch in her chest as she stared at him from across the room. Her gaze spoke volumes that she herself would never give voice to, and she was waiting for his answer as they stared at each other. She knew she should look away, do something else. But that would break the spell, and it was a lovely, intoxicating magic to behold.

Moments slipped by before Hank picked up his tools and completed hanging the last of the lights. Julie didn't move, knowing he would come to her. They each felt it, and both were powerless to stop it.

Hank stepped down and strode toward her purposefully. He surprised her when he reached out with the gentlest of touches and stroked her face.

Closing her eyes, she leaned into his caress. Hank's hand went around to the back of her neck, his touch tingling on her skin like the lightest of raindrops. Julie opened her eyes, and seeing the desire she felt mirrored in his eyes, leaned toward him to enjoy the kiss that his talented fingers promised.

He drew her inside the circle of his arms. Their mouths met hungrily as hands skated over each other, exploring.

His beard raked over her smooth skin, leaving a trail of sensation in its wake. She could feel the evidence of how much he wanted her, and reveled in her own power to excite this man.

Someone coughed near the stairway, and the couple sprang apart. Julie turned her back in embarrassment when she saw the man standing there.

"Hank William Jared, I thought I told you not to go kissing girls in my church basement," he said with a thick Irish brogue. Tall and thin, he had white hair and an athletic build that contrasted with his heavily lined face.

"I must have forgotten," said Hank, shaking the older man's hand with a boyish grin. "Father McHale, I'd like you to meet Julie Trueblood. He reached for her arm, spinning her around. Julie, this is Father

McHale. He's the priest who'll be marrying Kelly and Ron today."

A priest!

Julie wanted to melt into the concrete floor beneath her and die an invisible death. She heard herself say politely, "It's nice to meet you, Father."

To his credit, he didn't seem at all uncomfortable at having caught them in such a compromising position. "I'm also the priest who heard Hank William's first confession, when he was just a wee lad. I'm there in the confessional every Saturday, by the way." He rocked forward and back, with his hands behind him. "Or if you two are serious, perhaps we can have us a double ceremony." He winked conspiratorially at Julie.

I wish I was dead.

Father McHale looked around at the fully decorated church basement. "I must say, this looks wonderful."

"Thank you," they said in unison.

"Oh, and Hank, your mother called. She'd like you to call her back. Seems your cell phone must not get a signal down here."

"Son of a..." he pulled out his cell phone. "Sorry, Father. I've been waiting for an important call."

"I must be on my way. I have to see about building a roulette wheel for Monte Carlo night," said the priest. "I'll see you both at the ceremony." He walked back up the steps.

"Can I meet you in the parking lot, Julie? I need to see if Chip called."

"Sure. I'll be right there."

By the time she made it to the car, Hank was behind the wheel with the engine running.

"Is everything okay?" she asked.

"I missed his call."

"Did he leave a message?"

When he didn't answer, she thought she was being presumptuous. "It's none of my business."

"It is your business." He backed out of the parking spot. "His wife had the twins. They're fine, but she hemorrhaged after the birth."

"Oh, my God. Is she going to be okay?"

"They're not sure yet."

That wasn't all Chip had said on his message, but it was all Hank was prepared to share. The rest, he was going to pretend he never heard.

JULIE GAZED AT her reflection in the mirror and bit her lip. The dress was a deep blue silk that clung to her body in the most flattering of places, grazing her hips and cinching in tight under her accentuated breasts. The skirt billowed out around her legs with a feminine flourish, stopping just above her shapely ankles.

While the neckline and hem were modest, the dress

was racier that Julie would have liked for a wedding. She vaguely remembered Hank telling her to pack something appropriate, but she was crazy out of her mind after seeing the footprints leading from the barn. She had reached into the closet and grabbed several dresses, figuring one of them would be fine.

She glanced wistfully at the other two outfits that hung in the closet. The first was a safe and boring pink sundress, which would have been perfect if it were June instead of December. The second was a blazer and skirt combination that was far better suited to a funeral or job interview—perhaps a job interview at a funeral parlor—than a celebration of love.

Which left the dress she was wearing. Flaunting might be a better word.

No one will be looking at me anyway, except Hank.

At the thought, she relaxed her shoulders and tried to see herself as Hank would see her. Twirling slightly and smiling at her reflection, Julie's fears were confirmed. This dress had no business at a wedding. Unless maybe it was worn by the bitter ex-girlfriend of the groom.

There was a soft rap on the door. "May I come in?" asked Gwen.

"Yep."

Gwen's mouth dropped open. "You look incredible!"

"I look like a French whore."

"You most certainly do not." She grabbed Julie's arms and held them out to her sides. "You look like a fine and cultured woman, who just happens to have a glorious body."

Julie felt the first stirrings of pride at Gwen's assessment. She turned toward the mirror and twisted to see the back of the dress in the mirror. "You don't think it's too much?"

"Well, it is breathtaking. But Kelly's a fine-looking young woman and I don't expect you'll be stealing the bride's thunder, so to speak."

"It wasn't the bride I was worried about."

"Ah. Hank." Gwen gave Julie a conspiratorial smirk. "It might be a bit too much for Hank."

"I'll wear the pink one," Julie said, reaching for the mundane sundress. "Maybe Kelly or Marianne has a sweater I can put over…"

"I said it may be too much for Hank. I didn't say you should change."

"I'm not comfortable."

"On second thought, you're right. You should change. You wouldn't want that tall, dark and incredibly sexy man to lust after you."

Julie slowly turned from the closet, one hand on the pink sundress. "You think he'd lust after me if I wore this?" she asked, looking down at the blue silk number and brushing an imagined piece of lint off its fine surface.

"Definitely."

"Well," she said, peeking at herself in the mirror, "he is my boyfriend."

"You want him to be happy, of course. I just love weddings," she said wistfully. "Don't you?"

Julie nodded as she walked to the dresser and began brushing her hair. "I remember your wedding, Gwen. It was beautiful."

"It was."

If ever two people complimented each other, it was David and Gwen. They had made a striking couple—she with her curling blonde hair, smooth complexion and soulful blue eyes, he like a sandy-haired Greek god, all muscle and sinew.

"Did I ever tell you how we met?" asked Gwen.

Julie squinted her eyes. "No, I don't think so."

Gwen sat down on the bed. "I was living in New York City. The first time I saw him, he was sitting on an upside-down milk crate in Hell's Kitchen, holding a cello and a bow. I figured he was a street musician."

She had a far-away look in her eyes as she continued. "A red-headed girl was coming toward him from the opposite direction, and she asked him if he was going to play. 'Not right now,' he said, and she says, 'No one will give you money if you just sit there.'" Gwen laughed.

"He told her he didn't want anyone to give him money, he was just listening to the music of the street. I remember I loved how he said that."

"Wasn't he a composer?"

She nodded. "For movies, mostly. I was getting close to them now, and he turned to me with this beautiful smile and said, 'Would you like to hear a song?' Before I could answer, the red-head says, 'I thought you weren't going to play.' And I'll always remember," she said, putting her hand to her heart, "he said, 'That was before the most beautiful woman in the world tried to walk right by me, and all I had to stop her was a cello.'"

Julie sat next to her aunt, placing her arm around Gwen's shoulders. "That sounds just like him."

Gwen nodded, reaching up to hold Julie's hand. "We were inseparable after that. We never spent a single night apart, not from that very first day."

"Do you think you'll ever get married again?"

She shook her head. "No."

"Why not?"

"It's like that old saying. Lightning doesn't strike the same place twice. It was unbelievable that it happened the first time. I'm certainly not expecting it to happen again."

6

"SON OF A bitch!" Hank swore, shaking his injured index finger. "I have an idea," he said sarcastically, "let's use a giant, three-inch needle to hold a little tiny flower onto our jackets."

"Let me help," said Marianne. She took the pin and expertly attached the boutonnière to the lapel of his tuxedo on the first try.

Feeling like an awkward teenager, Hank gave her a pained grin. "Thanks, Ma."

"You're welcome," she said, brushing at the fabric of his tuxedo. "Now where's Kelly? We have to get this show on the road or the groom is going to beat us to the church!"

"If he shows up," Hank said under his breath.

"That is not funny."

"Of course it's funny." He looked at his mother as if she were crazy, earning him a playful slap on the back of his head.

Marianne walked to the stairway. "Kelly, we have to go!"

A pair of white pumps emerged onto the landing of the staircase. Kelly's dress was pure white, its length held up in her hands as she descended the stairs, exposing a layer of tulle. The fabric glistened with fine beading and just a touch of shimmering iridescent sequins, spread in clusters throughout the skirt. The bodice was strapless, its fabric wound in an elaborate knot that fell in a sweetheart neckline, complimenting her figure. As her glowing face came into view, Hank could see she wore her hair up in a fancy and delicate style, her only jewelry a shimmering purple stone on a fine gold chain.

"Oh, Kelly." His mother was crying. He could hear it in the tone of her voice. "You look wonderful." She held her youngest daughter. "My baby's getting married."

"I love you, Mom."

"I love you, too."

Kelly made a strangled little sound. "I miss Dad."

"Me, too." Marianne released her and squeezed her upper arms.

Kelly nodded and wiped at her eye makeup. Hank swallowed the knot that was forming in his throat and opened the last remaining box from the florist. Inside was a large teardrop bouquet of bright yellow roses and purple poppies.

His father had tended a yellow rose bush in the backyard for twenty years, just so he could share the blooms with his wife. The flowers reminded all the Jared children of their dad.

Hank handed the bouquet to his sister and kissed her gently on the cheek. "You look beautiful, Kelly."

"Thanks."

"Last chance," he said, determined to lighten the mood. "You want me to get you the hell out of here?" he smiled at his kid sister, so grown up and gorgeous. "No questions asked. I'll take you to Disneyland, Tahiti, wherever you want to go."

Kelly grinned despite her tears. "Nope."

"You sure?"

"Yep."

"Okay then." Hank gave his sister a tight squeeze. He lifted his head and saw Julie standing in the doorway, her hair falling in soft curls around her slender shoulders, the blue dress flowing along her body, and his heart stopped beating. "Wow."

Julie blushed. "Do you like it?" She raised her arms and spun in a circle.

"You look amazing."

She walked over to him and planted a kiss right on his lips. "Thank you."

Hank's eyes went dark as he snaked an arm around her waist and held her against him. "You're welcome," he said softly.

"All right, you two. Get in the car. We are going to be on time," Marianne said with purposeful optimism. Despite her firm tone, a secretive smile graced her lips as she ushered Hank and Julie out the door.

THE WAY JULIE saw it, she had one single day to be Hank Jared's girlfriend, and she was damn sure going to make the most of it.

"Can I get you anything?" he asked.

It was the second time Hank had come by the table where Julie and Gwen's sat. Julie was disappointed when she realized they weren't sitting together, but soon discovered the separation gave them a chance to stare at each other across the crowded room like they were in the high school cafeteria.

Each time she caught his eye, she felt brazen and bold; each time she caught him watching her, she was excited and unnerved.

"I think we're good. Your mother is an incredible cook," said Julie.

"This gravy is positively scrumptious," agreed Gwen.

"I'm going to move to this table after I dance with Kelly."

"You don't need to, Hank," said Julie. She didn't want to disrupt the wedding in any way.

"I want to." He looked at her, his face clearly showing her he spoke the truth, and she got a funny feeling in her stomach. "Kelly doesn't mind," he added, correctly guessing the reason for her refusal.

"Okay then."

"Sure I can't get you a drink?"

"Kamikaze, on the rocks," said Gwen, reaching between them and handing Hank her empty glass.

"You got it, lady."

"On second thought, I will take a drink. Something fruity and tropical."

"Coming right up." Hank walked to the bar and Julie's eyes followed him all the way there.

"My boyfriend has a great butt."

"Indeed."

The dinner music was an eclectic mix of 70s and 80s pop, and Julie's brow furrowed when Tommy Tutone's 867-5309 began to play.

"What's the matter?" asked Gwen.

"Every time I hear a number, I think I should try it in the cipher. Not because I think it will work, but because I have absolutely no idea what will."

"You'll know when it's the right one." Gwen took a sip of her water. "Doesn't it have to be thirteen digits or something?"

Julie shrugged. "Not really. If a key isn't long enough, you just put the leftovers in order at the end. Like for 867-5309, it doesn't have a one, two, four, ten, eleven, twelve or thirteen in it. So those numbers would go at the end."

"Isn't that clever."

"It works the same way for word keys. Take the letters of the alphabet that aren't in the keyword and tack them on at the end of the word, in alphabetical order."

"Ladies and gentlemen," said the DJ, "may I call your attention to the front of the room, where Mr. and Mrs. Sorenson are about to cut the cake." James Taylor's "How Sweet It Is" came on in the background as Kelly and Ron fed each other wedding cake with guarded movements, laughing.

"I imagine a cultural anthropologist would be an interesting date to have at a wedding," said Gwen.

"Why is that?"

"Look at these crazy rituals we engage in. Feeding each other cake. The throwing of the garter and the bouquet. Makes me wonder where it all came from."

"I don't think they do the garter and the bouquet anymore."

"Aw, really?" Gwen's disappointment was obvious. "Why not?"

"Sexist maybe."

"Oh, pooh. Some people take themselves far too seriously."

Hank returned with the drinks.

"Thank you, dear." She whispered in Julie's ear, "I

was hoping to catch the bouquet, you know," then she winked.

In the end it was Ron who played dirty first, dabbing cake on the end of Kelly's nose. That move earned him an ear full of yellow fondant, and buttercream frosting on the better part of his tuxedo vest.

"I have to go get ready for my dance with Kelly. I'll see you ladies in a little bit."

"Break a leg," said Julie, leaning in to kiss him on the cheek.

"You two make a very handsome couple," said Gwen as he walked away.

"If only."

"If only? Why if only?"

Julie looked at her like she had amnesia. "We're not really together, remember? I was just thinking…" she let her voice trail off.

"That you wouldn't mind if he really were your boyfriend."

"Dangerous thought, right?"

"I think it's a splendid thought. Hank Jared is a good man. He's handsome, comes from a good family. What's so dangerous about that?"

"He's a Navy investigator."

"Oh, yes. And in your book, that's akin to being an errand boy for Satan."

Julie rolled her eyes. "I didn't say that. It's just that I don't know where his loyalties lie."

Gwen took a sip of her Kamikaze. "Do you think his interest in you extends beyond your ability to decode the cipher?"

"That's what I'm worried about. I don't know for sure."

"You don't trust him."

"No."

"Are you basing that on reality, today? Or are you basing it on your past experiences with officers in the Navy?"

Julie watched several guests posing for pictures at the next table. "Probably past experiences."

"It would be a shame to convict that man of crimes he hasn't committed, even if the only punishment is the impossibility of a real relationship between the two of you. You have the spark. I can see it. The chemistry between you is popping."

Julie fingered the spruce centerpiece. "You might be right." She dropped the foliage and stood, grabbing her purse. "I'm going to the ladies room. I'll be back."

"I'll be here."

Gwen took a sip of her drink, enjoying the tang of triple sec and lime. She usually chose to drink wine, but special occasions merited special pleasures, and there was nothing she enjoyed more than a wedding. True love—particularly between young people like Kelly and Ron—was a sheer joy to witness.

She could see the love between Hank and Julie,

too, glowing like the tiniest ember. If it was carefully fanned, its flames could roar to life and keep them toasty warm for years to come, but at this stage it was just as easily extinguished.

Gwen planned to do what she could to send careful breezes their way.

Her love for her niece was fierce and strong, and she had long hoped for Julie to find true love like she herself experienced with David.

She watched Ron and Kelly dance their first dance together, as her memory flashed back to a picnic in the mountains, off a trail she and David frequently hiked together not far from the house. They had eaten mangos, rice salad and stuffed radicchio, drinking ice cold sake from Japanese cups. They made love in the woods, their picnic blanket spread on the ground, their clothes littering the forest floor.

David Beaumont was beautiful a way that only young men can ever be, his sculpted runner's body lithe and agile, his skin at once both supple and rough. Gwen wondered now what her husband would have looked like at forty-five, the age he would be now had he lived. If he aged like his father, he would only have grown more handsome, with smile lines instead of wrinkles and streaks of light gray hair to accentuate his chiseled features.

"I'm back," said Julie.

Across the dance floor, the DJ stood with Hank

and Kelly. "Ladies and gentlemen, as most of you know, Kelly's father passed away several years ago, so he isn't here today to dance with his little girl. Hank Jared, brother of the bride, will be standing in his father's place." The crowd clapped quietly, as Luther Vandross' "Dance With My Father" began to play.

Julie tried not to cry as she watched Kelly struggle to do the same. Hank spoke to his sister, making her smile as he pulled her into his arms. Julie was spellbound by the lyrics of the song, grief for her own father rising up, choking her.

How lucky Kelly was to have Hank to lean on, to make her smile in the middle of such a difficult moment. Watching him talk to his sister as he gracefully moved her around the dance floor, Julie wished for that man with all the concentration and might of a child wishing on a star.

The song ended and Hank wrapped Kelly in a tender embrace before kissing her on the forehead and walking her back to her new husband. Julie watched him take his drink off the head table and make a beeline back to where she sat with Gwen. As he come closer, she stood to embrace him.

Hank held her, letting her be the first to let go.

"The song," he said.

Julie nodded.

"I'm sorry."

"No. Don't be. It was beautiful." She wanted to tell

him that Kelly was lucky to have him as a brother, but she was too choked up to get the words out. Hank's eyes met hers, then he kissed her on the forehead as he had done his sister, and she clung to him again, reveling in the comfort of his arms.

Lifting her head, she said simply, "Thank you." Then kissed him on the mouth, as if it was the most natural thing in the world. When they separated, their hands remained together.

"Would you like to dance?" asked Hank.

"No, not yet. I'm waiting for the Electric Slide."

"A girl after my own heart."

It wasn't long before the DJ played the wedding classic. Marianne stood and raised both hands to the sky, giving a loud holler as she headed for the dance floor. She pulled family and friends with her as she went, grabbing Hank by the arm and pointing in Julie's direction. He did as he was told, heading over to collect her, and she graciously met him halfway to the dance floor.

As they stepped and clapped in unison, Julie couldn't remember ever having so much fun at a wedding reception. Gwen's loud, "Boogie woogie woogie," could be heard over the music, making Julie laugh and smile so wide her face hurt.

None of this is real, she reminded herself. Like Cinderella at the ball, her greatest fantasy was doomed to disappear when the clock struck midnight, leaving this dream in tatters.

Enjoy the ball while you can. Especially that prince.

As if he could hear her thoughts, Hank caught her eye and smiled a wolf's grin. There was a promise therein, that he would come to her if she allowed it. Julie felt her heart leap, pulse pounding, breath coming fast. The music ended and Julie stared back at him meaningfully, then looked pointedly at the door that led out of the basement.

She went first, knowing he would follow.

The air outside was cool. It was warm for December, but she could still see her breath hanging in little puffs. Footsteps behind her and she turned around, almost lunging into Hank's waiting arms. Their mouths met hungrily, Julie struggling to get closer, pressing her body to his and angling her head to return his passionate kisses.

"I can't keep my hands off you." He kissed her neck and shoulder.

Julie was lost in him, the flavor of his mouth and the smell of his skin. Were they really standing in a church parking lot, making out like teenagers? She felt naughty and daring, the emotions only increasing her excitement. She lifted her head and ran her hands in his thick dark hair.

"I think I like being a convincing girlfriend," she said between kisses.

His mouth stilled against hers, his hands stopped

their exploration of her body, and he pulled back.

"Whoa." He reached behind his neck to remove her arms. "You sure had me fooled."

The tone of his voice set off warning bells in Julie's head, yet she didn't understand just what she had done. "What's the matter?"

"I'm not a toy, Julie."

"What?"

He rubbed his hand roughly along his lips. "I'm not here for your amusement."

She felt as if she'd been slapped. Hank knew they were just pretending. So why was he so angry? It wasn't like he was really hurt, because he didn't care about her one way or the other. This was all a façade.

"I'm sorry if I offended you," she said, bewildered. "I thought you wanted me to be convincing." Julie stood rigidly still, suddenly chilled by the cold night air.

"We should get back," said Hank, his jaw set.

Julie looked at him beseechingly, already missing their earlier closeness. She wanted to understand why he was upset, her scrambled thoughts not making any sense. She opened her mouth to speak, but couldn't decide exactly what to say.

The door behind her opened and Ron appeared. "There you are. Kelly's about to throw the bouquet. Marianne insisted I find you two."

"We'll be right there." The door closed behind Ron. Hank smiled widely and offered his arm. "Ready, honey?"

The sarcasm wasn't lost on Julie, and she pouted, narrowing her eyes at him. She could play this any way he liked. Unless he tried to kiss her again. *That would definitely not be happening.*

She mirrored his confident grin and took his arm. "Of course, sweetheart. I wouldn't miss it for the world."

He walked her inside and deposited her back at her table before walking off. Gwen smiled widely and handed Julie one of two full Kamikazes.

"Welcome back!" shouted Gwen over the increasingly loud music.

"Thanks," she said, taking a long swig of the potent cocktail.

"Lover's quarrel?"

"Something like that."

"You look like you've been making out in the backseat of a Chevy." Gwen laughed at her own joke, and Julie used her hands to try to straighten her hair.

It was no use. "I'm going to the ladies room." She stood up to leave just as Marianne came up behind them.

"All the single ladies! That means you two!" said Marianne.

Gwen hopped out of her chair with a flourish. "I'm ready."

"I was just going to the ladies room," said Julie.

"Nonsense, you look fine," said Gwen, steering her toward the dance floor as she winked at Marianne. "I just love the tossing of the bouquet. Such tradition! I'm so glad they don't mind being sexist."

"I think I'm going to be sick," said Julie, then she downed the rest of her drink in one long gulp. Shaking her head, she worked to change her attitude. Hank Jared was not going to ruin her evening. She did some boxing moves, bobbing and weaving. "Let me at 'em. Lookout, all you eligible bachelors!" She put her arm around Gwen as they made their way to the dance floor. "The Trueblood women are on the prowl!"

They took their place on the dance floor with several teenage girls, a beautiful brunette, three bridesmaids and a matronly woman with black frizzy hair. One of the bridesmaids turned and rolled her shoulder away from the onlookers as she covered her face.

Julie felt her pain.

The DJ played a drum roll, and Kelly turned her back to the dance floor.

Please, don't let me catch that damn thing.

Then it was airborne, ribbons trailing behind it like a missile's tail. The bouquet bounced off the clawing fingers of a bridesmaid and headed for the frizzy-haired woman, ricocheting off her bust and landing squarely in Julie's begrudging arms. She looked at the roses and pansies like they were a pipe bomb waiting to explode.

"Woo hooo!" screamed Gwen, laughing. "Way to go, Julie!"

ACROSS THE ROOM, Hank leaned on the bar and ordered a scotch on the rocks. Damn if she didn't look beautiful, clutching those flowers like she wished the ground would open up and swallow her whole. So sweet and innocent.

Too bad it's all an act.

"Looks like you have some garter-catching to do," said his mother, sitting down on a barstool beside him. "A glass of your best Chardonnay, please," she said to the bartender.

"I hear it's all mid-shelf. No cheap stuff, but nothing great," said Hank.

"Bastards," she answered, smiling. She squeezed Hank's hand. "Thanks for everything you've done for the wedding. Your father would be proud."

"Thanks, Ma."

"Trouble in paradise?"

He took a sip of his drink and chewed on an ice cube. "Didn't you hear? That was just a reasonable facsimile of paradise. Not the real thing."

"Looked pretty real to me."

Hank motioned to the bartender. "Julie is a fabulous actress."

"I see." Marianne squared her shoulders to face her son, her head tipped to the side. "It must be confusing for her, pretending to be your girlfriend."

"Why is that?"

"Because she has very real feelings for you."

Hank scowled at his mother. "I think you're mistaken."

"Hank," she said softly, "a woman can tell these things. And that young lady," she gestured to Julie across the room, "is completely taken with you."

When his mother walked away, Hank turned back to scan the room and saw her. She was standing with Gwen next to the dance floor, watching anxiously as the single men assembled for the throwing of the garter.

Ron made his way to the front of the dance floor, Kelly's garter in-hand, and some possessive instinct had Hank up and on his feet before he could think better of it. Julie caught his eye as he assumed his place in the group of men on the dance floor, bending his knees like a baseball player in the outfield.

"Don't worry, baby," he yelled to Julie. "I used to play shortstop."

Ron turned his back to the men and threw the garter over his shoulder, which bounced off the low ceiling and landed on the opposite side of the floor. A young blonde man snatched it up and held it in the air victoriously with a loud cheer.

Without missing a beat, Hank walked over and opened his wallet, handing him a hundred dollar bill and taking the garter as the crowd laughed and cheered.

Hank swung his prize around on one outstretched finger, eyeing Julie like a cat eyes a mouse. A warm flush spread from her face to her chest, and he realized he was excited to put the garter on her leg, even if a hundred people were watching.

Anything just to touch her.

A chair appeared in the middle of the dance floor, and the DJ ushered Julie to the seat. For a moment she hid her face behind the bouquet, then bit her lip and forced her hands down into her lap. The theme from Mission Impossible began to play and laughter erupted again.

Hank paced in front of her, planning his attack. Stealthily he walked toward her and kneeled, then he lightly stroked his finger along the blue silk up her knee, exposing her calf.

He uncrossed her legs and took off her shoe, feeling her anxiety in the way she held herself. When he surprised her by tickling her foot, she shrieked, the crowd laughing along with her. He slipped the garter onto her ankle and began inching it upward.

Julie shot him a warning look as he passed her knee, prompting him to look at the crowd for guidance. The hoots and hollers egged him on, as he knew they would. He pushed the lace and ribbon up onto her thigh, his eyes connecting with hers once again. As she looked at him, he felt her legs relax and open to him the slightest bit, the look on her face offering him the world.

Hank had never wanted a woman as much as he wanted Julie in that moment. He felt his fingers tremble. He gave the garter one last pull high on Julie's thigh, snapping it against her skin and watching her flinch. Then he retreated, pulling her dress back down as he went. He stood and helped Julie to her feet before he kissed her, his lips on hers clearly saying, *to be continued*.

7

SNOWFLAKES BEGAN TO fall as Kelly and Ron waved goodbye from the window of the white stretch limousine, a large "Just Married" banner hanging from its trunk.

Hank stood in the cold and watched the tail lights disappear into the night. Norah and Steve had headed home an hour earlier, anxious to get back to their lives in Boston.

That meant there was another bedroom available at the house, if he chose to use it. Hank suspected Julie would share his bed tonight if he asked her.

He knew it was wrong to sleep with someone he was protecting as an officer of the Navy, someone who might be involved in this case more than he would like. Hell, who was he kidding? She was definitely involved. It was just a matter of degree. Hank shivered in the cold and cursed the situation.

The church doors behind him opened and closed.

"Hi," said Julie.

And he knew.

Julie Trueblood had gotten under his skin, maybe even into his heart. How the hell had that happened? Why did it have to be this woman who affected him so strongly?

He turned to see her standing on the steps of the church, her blue dress swirling in a light breeze, snowflakes twirling in the air between them.

"Merry Christmas, Hank," she said, smiling lightly. "It's just after midnight."

He would remember this moment always—how she looked—how it tore him up inside. "Merry Christmas, Julie."

"Are you ready?"

"Yeah."

"Your mom needs some help loading up the car." Julie opened the church door and waited for him to come inside. "Kelly and Ron get off okay?"

Hank nodded. "They said goodbye."

"It was a good day," she said, smiling at Hank and resting her hand on his back as they headed downstairs together. "You did good, Hank."

"We all did." They reached the bottom of the stairwell and Hank held the door for her.

An hour later, the group walked into Marianne's kitchen. Julie slipped off her high heels and covered a yawn. "I'm exhausted."

"Me too. Let's go to bed," said Hank.

Julie's head snapped up at his suggestion. "I need a few minutes to unwind."

Marianne opened a cupboard and withdrew a round bottle. "Nightcap, anyone?"

"Chambord," said Gwen appreciatively as she pulled back a chair. "Absolutely."

"Yes, please," said Julie.

"Why not," said Hank, closing his eyes.

"If you're tired, you can go ahead," said Julie.

"I got my second wind."

Marianne stifled a laugh as she poured the drinks into cordial glasses. They were a heavy cut crystal in pale pink, each one shaped like a tiny vase.

"Marianne, these are precious," said Gwen.

"They were my mother's."

"Just lovely. Really."

Hank thought of the china cabinet in the dining room, chock full of crystal, and wondered how long the women were going to stay up.

Julie rubbed her neck with her hand, and Hank saw his opening, walking behind her to rub her shoulders. She made little sounds of pleasure as he worked her tired muscles, her skin warm and smooth beneath his strong hands.

"Sure you don't want to go to bed?" he whispered in her ear.

Julie straightened her shoulders abruptly and lightly shook off his hands. He stepped away, his ego stinging from her response.

"It has been a long day. I think I am going to go to bed," he said.

"Goodnight, Hank," said Julie sweetly.

Once upstairs, he undressed in a huff. Hank had wrestled with his conscience and fully committed himself to breaking the rules, only to realize that Julie had no intention of coming to bed with him.

What kind of game was she playing? It seemed her affection was directly related to the size of their audience. He shouldn't have listened to his mother. He had been right all along. Julie was playing the role he had asked her to play, and was not interested in a real relationship with him.

"Stupid, stupid, stupid," he said to himself as he stepped into the shower. He let the hot water run over his head and flow down his face before he grabbed a bar of soap and worked up a heavy lather on his arms and chest. His mind replayed their kisses outside the reception hall and his body responded to the memory.

Was she really just pretending? Hadn't she felt even a portion of what he felt?

The rest of his body got the same punishing treatment with the soap before he turned off the water and hastily dried his body. He was a grown man, damn it, and these games were making him crazy. Hank pulled on a clean pair of black briefs and considered grabbing a T-shirt and shorts out of deference to Julie.

She can close her damn eyes if she doesn't like it.

Throwing back the covers on the bed, he dropped onto the cold sheets and waited for her to come in. It was nearly an hour before she did—time that did nothing to improve Hank's mood. He watched as she closed the door as quietly as possible and tiptoed into the room.

"I was starting to think you were sleeping on the couch."

In the darkness he saw her straighten to her full height. "I was talking with your mom and Gwen."

"You were avoiding coming to bed with me."

She didn't answer him.

"Why, Julie?" His eyes were adjusted to the dim light of the room, and he saw her cross her arms over her chest as he waited for a response. When none came, he asked again, "Why are you avoiding me?"

She snapped at him. "Because you don't really like me anyway, and I don't want to sleep with someone who…"

"Whoa, wait a minute. I don't really like you anyway? What are you talking about?" Hank swung his legs out of bed and walked toward her.

She stepped backwards and bumped into a dresser.

"This whole charade. You pretending to like me."

"I do like you, Julie."

"No, not like that. Like a man likes a woman."

"I do like you like a man likes a woman."

"No," she said, shaking her head. "I'm not being very clear."

Hank reached out and stroked his hand down her arm.

"Please don't touch me," she said, recoiling. "I'm trying to make you understand."

"I understand. You think I don't like you like a man likes a woman, but you're wrong."

"I know you're attracted to me, Hank, and I'm attracted to you, too. That's not what I'm talking about."

Now he was confused. He furrowed his brow. "Go ahead."

"You want to have sex with me, but you don't really care about me."

Silence filled the room.

Julie let out a huff and moved to step around him.

His hand on her arm stopped her. "Wait." His fingers trailed slowly down her arm. "I do care about you." He stepped closer, his scent invading her senses. "Enough to get involved when every rule the Navy has, and every rule I have for myself, tells me not to."

His words lulled her closer, tempting her with their promise. Her shaking fingers skimmed his chest, reaching higher until her hand curved around his broad shoulder. With the lightest pressure she pulled him to her, his mouth finding hers with unerring accuracy in the darkness.

She tasted like berries and spicy mint, and Hank leaned into her. He thought he could remain unaffected, aloof, enjoying her body and the pleasure she offered without involving his heart. She brought him to a place he had never been before, where bodies melded and feelings entwined, inseparable from one another. They met on a battlefield, a firestorm of emotional victory and defeat, where he fought for self preservation and was beaten down, rising stronger, more powerful, having opened his heart to love.

JULIE HUMMED TO herself as she poured a cup of coffee. She had woken up in Hank's arms, the sunlight streaming in from the window, feeling content and happy. Carefully lifting his arm, she slipped out of bed and lowered the blinds so Hank could continue to sleep, then dressed and headed downstairs to see what the day held in store.

She had always been a morning person, enjoying the feeling of the entire day laid out before her. On the rare occasion she slept in, she usually felt sluggish and off her game. This morning, the house was deserted, and Julie didn't know if Gwen and Marianne were still sleeping or if they were doing other things. Gwen had little respect for time in general, and could be found sleeping or awake when least expected, so Julie had learned not to assume anything.

An unopened box of chocolate-covered doughnuts beckoned her, and she thought about helping herself to one or two. She was starving, and wondered if a night of passionate lovemaking was to blame for her terrific appetite. Her manners wouldn't allow her to open the doughnuts, so she rummaged through the cupboards until she found an already opened box of Lucky Charms.

She had loved that cereal since she was a little girl, though she only ever ate the marshmallows. Reaching for the box, a memory flashed through her mind.

Her mother was leaning over, a golden locket dangling from her neck to Julie's young face. "It's my good luck charm," she said.

"Why is it good luck?"

"When I was fourteen, I fell in love with your father. He was eighteen, and my mother wouldn't let me see him because he was so much older."

"He enlisted in the Navy, and he asked my parents if he could send me letters. He didn't want my mother to know what he was saying, so he wrote in code. Your father always loved codes," she laughed, fingering the locket.

"He used numbers to stand for letters in the alphabet, then he made pictures around the outside of the paper with dots. The number of dots in each line stood for that letter of the alphabet."

"That's so cool."

"Yes. My mother thought he was quite an artist, all those decorative lines around the page. Only I knew the truth. He hid his love for me in the designs on the page."

Julie fingered the locket, for the first time noticing the dimpled dots that comprised its decoration. "Is this a code?" she asked, mesmerized.

"It is."

"What does it say?"

"It says, 'Beautiful'." Her mother smiled and Julie thought she was indeed the most beautiful woman in the world.

Frantic now, Julie put down the box of cereal and searched the room for a piece of paper. She saw a magnetic notepad on the refrigerator and hastily reached for it.

Down the left-hand side she wrote out the letters of the alphabet; next to them she numbered one through twenty-six. Across the bottom she wrote BEAUTIFUL, then she wrote the corresponding number below each letter. Some of them were two digits. In the end, she was staring at thirteen individual numbers.

"Oh, my God, Oh, my God, Oh, my God," she whispered to herself, staring at what she knew was the key to deciphering the code from the safe deposit box. She needed to tell Hank. She turned to head for the bedroom when a cell phone on the counter in front of her began to vibrate. She glanced at the screen.

ADMIRAL BARSTOW

Time stood still. Julie was paralyzed, betrayal surrounding her like a thick smoke. The phone continued to vibrate as panic rose up like bile. Barstow was calling Hank, and there could only be one reason for that.

He really was an errand boy for the devil.

8

THE WOMEN STOPPED at a Wal-Mart for supplies and cash, taking out as much money as the ATM would allow and gathering the materials Julie needed to create the cipher wheel. Then they headed south in Hank's SUV.

Julie was sitting in the passenger seat, which was now parked an hour and a half away from Marianne's at the Albany airport. In her lap were twelve slices of a paper towel roll, each neatly marked into twenty-seven equal sections. The thirteenth was in her hand, along with the ruler and a pen. It was careful work, but she was nearly done.

A light green minivan pulled into the next parking spot over, and Gwen hopped out of its driver's side door. Julie finished the last of her measuring and climbed out to join her.

"I thought a minivan was more practical, in case

we needed somewhere to sleep."

"Good call."

The women worked to move their belongings and supplies to the new vehicle, Gwen once again taking her place at the wheel. She turned around in her seat to back out cautiously, then headed toward the interstate.

"Julie, I had to give them a credit card and a driver's license," she said.

"Crap."

"I know. But they wouldn't give me the van without it, and they wouldn't take the prepaid credit card. My license says Trueblood, but I had a MasterCard in the name of Gwen Beaumont, and she let me use that one when I pretended I had just gotten married and it was all I had."

"Wait, you took David's name?"

"I tried it on for size. I went back to Trueblood after a month or two." Gwen took a last sip of her soda, the straw taking in air with a loud slurp.

"Maybe the different name will be enough to throw them off." Julie said hopefully, though her voice sounded false to her own ears.

No use crying over spilled milk.

Julie inserted the battery into the disposable cell phone she picked up at Wal-Mart and held the power key, its display coming to life. She hit the internet browser button and immediately looked up the

Leopold Cipher.

"Are you almost done?"

"Close."

Each of the thirteen numbered rings would be labeled with all the letters of the alphabet on it and one blank, each in a different order. This is what she needed to look up, and she meticulously copied them from the internet site to the rings she had created. The key—the thirteen numbers she gleaned from "beautiful"—would tell her the order of the rings themselves.

"Nothing to it, but to do it," she said to herself. With shaking hands, she grabbed another roll of paper towels and slid the towels off it, then used the scissors to slice the cardboard open with one long cut.

"What's that for?" asked Gwen.

"I need a dowel to put the rings on. It has to be a little smaller in diameter than they are." She cut a long piece of duct tape and put the roll back together, with a sliver of itself tucked inside the roll.

"This is so exciting!"

Julie smiled at her aunt's enjoyment, her own stomach in knots. Digging in her pocket, she found the paper where she had written the cipher key and began to place the rings onto the long roll in the correct order.

"Now what?" asked Gwen.

"Now I turn the wheels to spell out the first thirteen letters of the coded message." Julie skipped over the first line, knowing that had only been a reference for her to know to use the Leopold cipher.

"You put the gibberish in?"

"Yes."

"How do you get the message out?"

Julie finished lining up the first thirteen letters of text, using a piece of tape to hold them in position. "You roll it around until you find the line that makes sense." As she spoke, she opened her palm and let the cipher wheel roll slowly down her fingers. Her eyes scanned line after line of gibberish before the words suddenly jumped out at her.

I AM NOT DEAD

She jerked her hand back as if she'd been burned, and the cipher roll fell to the floor of the van.

"Holy shit!" Julie snapped.

"What?"

"'I am not dead'! It says, 'I am not dead'!"

"Holy shit," said Gwen.

"My father is alive!"

HANK DIDN'T KNOW she was gone until lunchtime.

Since Julie put the blinds down, he slept until almost eleven. When he couldn't find her, he looked for the dogs and figured the women had taken them for a walk.

He sat alone at the kitchen table, sunlight streaming in the windows and a hot cup of coffee in front of him, planning his future with Julie Trueblood. It would be touchy, given her involvement in this case, but he had no intention of letting her go. Hank knew a good thing when it stared him in the face, and that woman was as good as it got.

He was in up to his knees emotionally. It wasn't just physical. Hell, they had rocked the physical world off its axis last night, but that alone wouldn't have him sitting here thinking about their future. His mind was telling him this might be the one he had waited his whole life for, and Hank was wise enough to embrace that possibility and not let it get away from him, no matter who their relationship might upset.

Barstow's going to shit his pants.

Hank smiled at the thought as he lifted his cereal bowl to drain the remaining milk. Still, he wanted to minimize the negative consequences that dating Julie could have on his career, and that was going to take some doing.

Marianne walked in, carrying several grocery bags. "Morning."

"Hey, Ma. Merry Christmas."

"Merry Christmas. I thought you were out."

"Why?"

"Because your truck's not here."

Hank's brows snapped together, then he stood up

and peered out the window.

"I do know what your truck looks like," said his mother sarcastically.

"Yeah. I know." He sat back down at the table and shrugged. "Julie must have taken it."

"Where is she?"

"I don't know. I just got up a few minutes ago. I thought she and Gwen took the dogs for a walk."

"In the truck?"

That was odd. There must be a good explanation for why the two of them, the dogs and the truck were all missing. "Did they leave a note?" He hadn't really looked for one. A sick feeling settled in the hollow of his stomach as Marianne scanned the counter tops, shaking her head.

"The pad is out, but no note."

She wouldn't just leave.

As if to prove it to himself, Hank walked to the pantry and looked inside, his eyes resting where the dogs' food had been since the women arrived.

It was gone.

Hank stared at the spot longer than necessary.

Julie was gone.

But why? It didn't make sense. He was working to keep them safe. What had changed to make them want to leave?

The only thing that had changed was a night of incredible sex. Was she running away from a relationship with him? Julie had not seemed upset by them taking things to the next level. On the contrary, she seemed as moved by what they had shared as he was.

Then what? What could possibly make them take off in his SUV like that?

An image of Julie flashed in his mind. *"Are you sure we're safe here?"*

Panic slammed into Hank and set him reeling, his eyes darting to doors and windows, locks and unbroken panes.

"Was anything out of the ordinary this morning?" he asked his mother.

"No, not that I noticed. Why?"

Hank's cell phone rang and he glanced at the caller ID. ADMIRAL BARSTOW was displayed across the screen in big blue letters. He could see Julie standing where he stood, seeing what he was seeing.

"Son of a bitch!" Hank smacked his hand down violently on the counter. "She saw my phone. Son of a bitch!" he screamed, pounding his fists as the phone continued to ring.

Marianne turned from her groceries and stared at her son.

"Jared," he nearly shouted into the receiver.

"Where the hell have you been? I've been calling all morning," said Barstow.

Any doubts about Julie's departure vanished in an instant. Julie and Gwen were running for their lives.

Running for their lives, from me.

"It's Christmas Day, sir," Hank bit off the words, barely restraining his frustration with the older man.

"What goddamn difference does that make?" he barked. "You work for me, Jared. Not forty hours. All the fucking time. Do I make myself clear?"

Hank fought against the desperate need to verbally rip apart his superior officer. He concentrated on breathing in and out, feeling the air fill his lungs, and heard himself say, "Of course, sir."

"Where are you on the McDowell case?"

"Julie's still working on the cipher."

"You're sure she would tell you if she solved it?"

Not anymore.

"Yes, sir."

"Do what you have to in order to earn her trust."

"What do you mean, sir?"

"I mean," Barstow chuckled, a dirty throaty noise that disgusted Hank, "she's a beautiful woman, Jared. She just lost her father and she's vulnerable. Do what you need to do to ingratiate yourself with her."

Hank felt nauseous and angry, self-loathing warring with indignation in his blood.

That's what Julie thinks I did. She thinks I betrayed her.

Barely trusting himself to speak, Hank didn't respond at all. In his mind, his fist connected with Barstow's face. It was all he could do to remain silent.

"One more thing."

"What?"

"What the hell are you doing at the Albany airport?"

"Sir?"

"Don't play with me, son. Now, I'd like to know," he drawled out, "why you're touring the goddamned Northeast without updating me on this fucking case. I shouldn't have to call you to find out your fucking flight itinerary. Do you understand me, Jared?"

Realization dawned clear. "You have a GPS on my car."

"Of course I do." The admiral snickered. "And you'd better start explaining."

"I REMEMBER HER," said the young man at the rental car counter. He had a swatch of dyed blonde hair amidst masses of brunette curls. "Did she do something wrong?" He held his hand to his chest, wide-eyed.

Hank had been showing Julie and Gwen's pictures around to ticket agents and car rental employees for nearly an hour. It had taken thirty-five minutes to have their pictures sent from DMV in the first place.

"When was she here?"

"Just before lunch. Let me pull up the transaction." He typed efficiently into his computer. "Eleven twenty-two. She rented a light green Honda Odyssey. What did she do?"

"I'll need the license plate number."

"Of course." He leaned over the counter and whispered, "Was it a robbery? There was a bank robbery right down the street last week."

"No." Hank looked at his watch, which read 3:34. They had more than a four hour jump on him. At least they were driving, not halfway to Mexico on an airplane.

"It has Illinois plates, number F73 8M1. I'll write that down for you." He grabbed a purple sticky note and looked at Hank from under his lashes. "Did she skip bail? I won't tell anyone."

"I can't discuss the details. Thanks for your help."

He straightened and handed Hank the paper. "Is there anything else I can do for you today, sir?"

"No, that's all."

He pulled back the note before Hank could grab it. "Airport security has surveillance footage, if that would be helpful."

"Really?"

The clerk nodded, allowing him to take the paper, then leaned over again and whispered dramatically, "Was it a *murder*?"

THE AIRPORT SECURITY office was small and outfitted with a limited supply of dated equipment. Hank sat in the darkened room as a white-haired man in a blue uniform shirt held down a fast forward button on what looked like an old VCR.

"There's one more feed from the south parking lot," he said.

Julie must have parked in the quadrant of the parking garage not covered by the first three tapes Hank watched. He rubbed his forehead against the throb that was beginning to take over.

Just when he was convinced that this tape was yet another dead end, he saw his SUV pull right in front of the camera. "That's it," he told the security officer. "That's the truck."

The officer rewound the tape and began again, when the truck first entered the camera's field of view. Hank could clearly see Gwen driving, and as she pulled in, Julie sitting in the passenger seat. What were those things in her lap?

He watched as Gwen got out of the truck, presumably to go rent the minivan. Julie remained behind, working on something.

"Can we zoom in and see what she's doing?"

The other man pressed buttons on the archaic machine, and the image on the screen became cropped and grainy. "Is that better?"

"No."

The security officer laughed. "It's not like you see in the movies, is it?"

Hank thought of all the high tech security equipment he was used to dealing with, but kept that to himself. "No, it's not." He watched on screen as Julie wrote something, unable to see exactly what she was doing. Ten minutes later, Gwen returned with the van.

It wasn't until Julie threaded the rings onto the new paper towel roll that he realized what she was making.

The cipher wheel. She must have broken the code!

But when? She had trusted him up until this morning. If she had discovered the key before then, she would have told him. It must have been right around the same time as Barstow's call, maybe even at Marianne's house.

Hank dialed as he continued to watch the screen. "Ma. The notepad on the counter. Use a crayon or a pencil or something to see if you can read what was written on it last."

"Hang on, let me find a pencil." There was a long pause. "There are all these letters and numbers down the side… then the word 'beautiful' at the bottom with some numbers written under it."

Hank bent his head in a moment of gratitude to the universe. "Read them to me," he said to his mother.

His next call was to Chip Vandermead, though he hated to call him when Melody wasn't doing well. He answered on the first ring. Hank told him it was the Leopold Cipher and that the keyword was beautiful. It took Chip only moments to plug the information into his computer.

I AM NOT DEAD
I CAN PROVE MY INNOCENCE
BUT NEED YOUR HELP
MEET ME AT UNCLE LEOS

Chip was even able to cross-reference McDowell with Leo, pulling up several hits in the case file of one Leo Basinski, an immigrant from Uzkapostan whose last known address was just outside of Washington, D.C.

THE HIGHWAY WAS virtually deserted, given the lateness of the hour and the holiday. Hank made his eyes wide and blinked several times to say focused on the road. His mind kept going back to the hotel room in Jacksonville, with a body in the bathtub that someone now wanted him to believe *was not* Commander John McDowell.

Why had been so quick to assume it was his body in the motel room in the first place? Without positive identification, it was a bad judgment call on his part to have jumped to that conclusion, no matter how obvious it seemed at the time.

Sloppy. That's what it was.

One fact remained. Commander McDowell was involved in this case somehow. He might even have been the one to shoot the John Doe in the bathroom, or set the fire. Maybe both. And who was the dead man, if not the commander himself?

Hank thought of Julie, no doubt elated by her father's miraculous rise from his assumed grave. For her sake, he hoped McDowell was innocent of any wrongdoing and would find a way back into her life.

He doubted it, but he hoped.

A black and white checkered flag on the GPS screen showed he was getting close to his destination.

Protocol said he should have called Barstow about Leo, but now that the admiral was flying blind without that GPS, Hank wanted to keep him in the dark. No way in hell was he tipping his hand until he knew for sure Barstow wasn't a threat to Julie.

LEO WASN'T REALLY her uncle. Julie vaguely remembered him from her childhood as a short, dark-haired man with glasses, who wore too much cologne. Their family would have brunch at Leo's restaurant every month or so, with the occasional dinner at his home.

Her eyes scanned the row of brownstones, many decorated with Christmas lights for the holiday. The women walked in the road until they reached a shoveled driveway, allowing them access to the sidewalk without stepping through snow. Several doors down, a particularly frightening iron gargoyle sat atop a stone pillar, just as it had in Julie's childhood.

"I always hated that thing," she said, reaching it

and pausing to consider its gruesome mouth and fangs.

"It really isn't befitting the architecture, is it?" asked Gwen.

The women climbed the steps to the door and Julie knocked, exchanging a nervous glance with Gwen as she did.

"Maybe no one's home," said Gwen.

Julie shook her head. "I can hear the TV."

"Knock louder."

At Julie's uncomfortable look, Gwen stepped forward and pounded on the door. A moment later, a bald man with thick glasses and a hunched gait opened it. He stood before them, staring at Julie for too long without speaking.

"I don't know if you remember me. I'm Julie, John McDowell's daughter."

"I know." Said the old man, coughing loudly. It was a thick sound, and it made Gwen grimace.

"Is my father here, Leo?"

He glared at Gwen.

"This is my aunt, Gwen Trueblood."

Leo shook his head.

"Why not?" asked Julie.

He opened his mouth to speak and coughed several times instead. When he could manage, he said, "Just you."

"It's okay," said Gwen, turning to face Julie. "You can do this without me."

Julie nodded, taking strength from her aunt's words.

"I'll be in the car."

Leo waited until Gwen was back inside the vehicle before he stepped back for Julie to enter.

The small room was stale with the smell of boiled vegetables and cigar smoke, its blinds closed to the outside. An overly loud, outdated television played *Wheel of Fortune.*

"In the basement," he said, leading the way through a tiny dining room with a bowl of fake fruit and a built-in corner hutch.

Leo opened a narrow door, gesturing for her to go ahead.

The stairway was poorly lit, and Julie held on to the low handrail as she navigated the steep steps. Leo closed the door behind her, cutting the meager light in half and making her start. Her feet stopped moving as she gave her eyes time to adjust to the darkness. There was a smell of damp earth and something foul that Julie couldn't place. She began to descend again, the temperature dropping with each step down.

As she slowly made her way to the basement, she couldn't help but feel she was headed underground like the damned. This was not a place of resurrection, fresh and new, but a place of desperation and despair. She realized with fear that her father might not be here at all, and resisted the urge to turn back.

In her mind she saw a picture of her father, dead in a motel room. She hadn't been able to really believe he was dead until this very moment, when she was just steps away from the promise of him alive.

What the hell's the matter with me?

Ahead of her, the staircase ended on a square wooden landing. A wall of packed earth faced her, a thick invasive root visible in the densely packed clay. Julie neared the bottom step and her head lowered enough to see the basement. Time itself stopped moving, the air around her fixed and still.

A slick smile spread across his lips. "I knew you'd come," he said.

—9—

GWEN SAT IN the green minivan staring at the light over Leo's door. The bulb was yellow, making his doorway standout from every other on the street in an odd display of color. Another person would have thought nothing of that light, but it bothered Gwen like an ice cube that doesn't float to the top of the glass.

Something isn't right inside that house.

She considered knocking back on that door and attempting to talk her way past Leo, but her gut told her to stay put—at least for now. She tapped her foot with uncharacteristic nervous energy and waited, whether for Julie to return or for the decision to go in after her, she didn't know.

Her mind wandered over her beloved niece. Gwen was fiercely protective of the woman she had become, and knew Julie's heart was fragile where her father was concerned. John McDowell had never worked especially hard to spare his daughter pain, and it was with great effort that Gwen had kept her dislike of the man a secret from Julie.

She remembered with lucidity the teenager she had taken in when John abandoned his daughter. Gwen had been on her own emotional journey after David's death, unsure at the time if she could provide the girl with what she would need to heal.

Julie had been devastated, grief for her mother still oozing and raw, before her father left her as well. In his wake, a formal investigation followed that soon focused exclusively on her as a potential colluder, or at the very least, a threat to national security.

Gwen stood steadfast by her side, fending off Navy investigators and media reporters like wolves at the door, working to help Julie keep from shutting down emotionally. Teaching her to trust her own instincts, rely on herself again. Together they spent hours just talking, often walking through the Vermont hills that surrounded the farmhouse.

On one of their walks, a year after Julie's arrival, they came across a mother deer and her fawns grazing in an open meadow. Gwen's big yellow dog was grazing in the grass alongside them.

"Well, would you look at that," said Gwen. "It looks like Zeke has made some new friends."

The women watched the scene in silence for some moments.

"It's like us," said Julie. "You're the deer, and I'm the dog."

Gwen tilted her head. "What do you mean?"

Julie looked at the ground and frowned. "You took me in like I belonged with you."

Gwen had thought she might weep for this brave girl who felt so alone. "You do belong with me, sweetheart." She put her arm around Julie's shoulders. "We're family."

The memory brought a tight smile to her lips as she stared at Leo's brownstone. John McDowell was also Julie's family.

He hadn't always been so selfish. Gwen remembered when he first married her sister, he had been charming and strong. He loved Mary. It was her death that had changed him, made him angry and bitter.

Why did you bring us here, John?

Gwen bowed her head before the divine, praying for guidance and the safety of those she loved. When she raised it again, the yellow light over Leo's door had begun to flicker irregularly. She drew her lips into a pucker and curled her fingers around the steering wheel. Slowly and deliberately, she filled her lungs completely with air and focused all her energy on her niece.

THE GUN WAS the first thing Julie saw, her eyes drawn

to its shiny metal butt sticking out of the holster.

John McDowell stood before his daughter in a dirty T-shirt and green sweatpants, the weapon held by leather straps that were meant to be concealed beneath a jacket.

"Dad?" Her voice was ragged, her throat constricted.

"Julie-girl," he said, his arms open wide to receive her.

It was a scene she had imagined so many times before, it felt surreal when she finally ran the few steps into his arms. "I thought you were dead," she choked on a sob.

"I know. I'm sorry."

Julie released him, stepping back and wiping away the tears that wet her face. "I can't believe you're really here," she said. "It's so good to see you."

"It's good to see you, too." His tone was placating, as if he had simply left the room for a few minutes, rather than disappearing for ten years.

Julie took a good look at her father. His hair, once a salt-and-pepper black and gray, was now completely black, like it was when she was little. The youthful color contrasted with the deeply set lines around his mouth and the sagging of the skin under his dark-colored eyes.

She took in his clothing, her brow furrowing at his bare feet.

Where are his shoes? He's always so meticulous about his shoes.

He was at once both comfortingly familiar and unsettlingly strange. Julie ran a trembling hand through her hair as she looked at the room around them. It was set up like a small studio apartment, its dirt floor covered with a braided rug. A sagging couch was draped in tired pink fabric, next to a bed with striped yellow and brown sheets.

A power strip hung in mid-air, suspended from an orange electrical cord reaching down from the ceiling above. Julie's eyes followed the lines to a small refrigerator and a computer on a makeshift desk.

The overall feel was one of a bomb shelter or tomb, the earthen walls enhancing the sense of being buried alive. Julie shivered and wished for a window or door.

"How long have you been living here?"

"I don't know. A few months."

She tried to imagine anyone choosing to stay in this place a single moment longer than necessary. "Where did you live before that?"

"What?" He squinted at her.

"Where did you live before that?"

He began to pace between the desk and the couch. "What difference does that make?"

"It's okay, Dad. Never mind." Julie rubbed her eyebrow. "Your message said you could prove your innocence, but you needed my help."

A smile graced his face, brightening his features as he brought his chin up. "I do need your help, Julie-girl."

"Anything, Dad."

He blinked repeatedly. Julie saw little dots of sweat collecting on his forehead.

"You have to believe me."

The urge to run out of the basement and away from her father appeared suddenly, frightening in its intensity. She could see herself darting around him to make it to the stairs, clay walls under her fingertips as she raced up the steps, reaching the front door before Leo could even stand up from the couch and *Wheel of Fortune*.

Can opener.

"What is it?" she asked instead.

"Do you remember when your mother told you she had cancer?"

"Yes." She took a step backwards, increasing the distance between them. Her father stepped forward.

"You asked me that day, 'Why did she get sick?' Do you remember that?"

"I remember being upset," Julie swallowed against the dryness in her throat, an image of her beautiful mother forming in her mind.

"You asked me why she got sick. And I didn't tell you the truth." He was standing so close to her, she could smell his sweat.

"It was a rare form of cancer." Julie said, mechanically repeating the words she'd been told.

"Yes. A rare form of cancer that you only contract if you're exposed to ionizing radiation."

"Ionizing radiation?"

"Yes."

"Where would she be exposed to that?"

"At Camp Harold." He stepped away from her, cool air rushing in to fill the space he had occupied.

Julie's mother had been a Navy structural engineer, working at the same base as her father. The two had married on the base. Her mother had died on the base.

"When she was diagnosed, that goddamned Navy doctor said it was just one of those things that happens. Bullshit. I looked into it. It's caused by ionizing radiation from TENORM in the concrete on the worksite. They knew it was there." His body contorted in rage. His nostrils flared with each breath and his clenched arms shook. "They knew all along."

He turned to the fridge and grabbed a beer, opening it and drinking it down in one long gulp before pitching it into a tall white garbage can. The sound of it hitting other empties punctuated the silence before he opened the fridge and found a replacement.

"You want to know why your mother's body is rotting in the ground? The U.S. Navy killed her, sure as I'm standing in front of you."

Julie recoiled from the image he painted. "One or

two people made a bad decision…"

"Not *one or two*," he said derisively. "It ran all the way up the chain of fucking command, right to the Pentagon. Nobody said diddly! That's what killed your mother. The U.S. Navy, and the absolute authority it holds over the people enslaved by it."

He stood shock-still, staring at one of the electrical cords hanging from the ceiling. "They killed the only person I have ever loved."

I love you, Daddy.

The words rang out in her head, unbidden.

"But I got those fucking bastards."

She watched him suckle at the can of beer as a light humming began to sing in her ears. Then it clicked.

He really is a traitor.

"The Dermody." She wasn't asking for confirmation. She knew it now. For ten long years she had suffered for him, believing this man was an innocent victim. Eighty-eight men had perished when that ship went down.

John McDowell had killed them all.

A cold sensation trickled down from the top of her head to her abdomen. Julie stole a peek at the stairway, now seeming so much farther away. It was too late to make excuses and leave unquestioned; the opportunity for safety had passed untaken.

Her father was waiting. Julie said a silent prayer. *Please get me out of here. Help me get back to Hank. I think I love him. I shouldn't have doubted him.*

Julie heard the drip of water nearby. She listened as she counted the drops, one, two, three. Her lungs filled with air, calming her, and she knew what she had to do.

"Thank you, Dad."

"For what?"

She reached out to him. "For taking good care of mom," she said, squeezing his arm. "For getting the people that did this to her."

A proud smirk appeared on his face. He lifted the beer can and finished the rest of the brew. Tilting it toward Julie, he asked, "Oh, I missed you, Julie-girl. Do you want one?"

"Absolutely." Her palms were soaked with perspiration. "You said you needed my help. What can I do, Dad?"

"I'm still working covert ops for Uzkapostan." He puffed his chest as he spoke. "Been living there since I left the states. Once the Navy fucked me, I figured there's no place like home, right?"

Julie tried to keep up with his quick change of mood.

"So anyways, they've been getting weapons from the Navy for years. They had a backstage all-access pass to the U.S. Navy supply arsenal, via their own invisible account on the network."

The technology maven in Julie was horrified.

"That's awesome."

"It was, it truly was, until somebody shut it down six months ago. I need you to get us back into that database."

Only a handful of people in the world could do that, and Julie knew she wasn't one of them. "Anything for you, Dad."

"I would do anything for you, too. Do you know that?"

I'd sink a whole ship full of sailors for you, baby.

"Yes, Dad."

He smiled like a child who couldn't keep a secret. "That boyfriend of yours, Greg?"

The hair on the back of Julie's neck went up. "Yes?"

"He was sent to bring you back to do this."

"What?"

He waved off her excitement. "I have always been so proud of you. I told everyone who would listen how my girl was a natural-born code breaker. They thought it would be too dangerous if I came back here myself, so they sent Greg to come get you."

Dizziness crept into the back of Julie's brain, her father's words beginning to ring like church bells in her mind. "They sent Greg?"

"Yeah." His expression turned dark and ominous. "Fucking hotshot thought he could do this without me. Bring you back himself and take me out of the loop."

His laugh was too loud, his happiness pronounced. "I took care of that dumb ass son of a bitch."

"The motel," she whispered.

The body in the bathtub was Greg.

"You know about that?"

Julie battled the sick fear that made her want to double over. "Of course. The code in the safe deposit box. That's how they found me."

"Oh, right. Yeah, right. He wasn't good enough for you, Julie. We'll find you somebody real good when we get home. A nice Uzkapostan boy like your old man."

"We're going to Uzkapostan?"

"Tomorrow morning. The same flight Greg was going to take you on."

"I don't have my passport."

He flashed her a cocky smile. "Oh, yes, you do. I got it from your apartment."

WITH AN EERIE sense of déjà vu, Hank ducked under the yellow police tape and approached the smoldering building. A guttural scream rose in his chest and begged to be freed as he walked closer to the brownstone and the familiar smell of waterlogged timber.

No. No. No.

"Sir, you need to step behind the barrier."

He flashed his badge. "Who's in charge?"

The fireman nodded to a woman standing beside a

large red SUV. He identified himself, his hands shaking as he flashed his badge and asked, "What do we have here?"

"Explosion. Appears to have been deliberately set, probably natural gas. One confirmed dead."

He could feel his chin trembling. "Male or female?"

"Male. From the neighbor's description, it appears to be the owner, Leo Basinski."

Hank pressed his palms to his eyes and nearly wept with gratitude.

"You okay, mister?"

"Yes. I thought it was a friend." He took a big breath. "Was there anyone else in the building?"

"Negative. Neighbor says he lived alone."

Hank's cell phone vibrated in his pocket. He fished it out and saw an unfamiliar number with an 802 area code.

Vermont.

He stepped away from the SUV. "Hank Jared."

"It's Gwen."

"Thank God. Where are you guys?"

"Julie's not with me."

"Where is she? I'm sitting outside Leo Basinski's house, watching them carry him out in a plastic bag, Gwen. What the hell's going on?"

"Oh, my God. We were just there!"

"Where's Julie?"

"She's with her father. I'm following them, Hank. Ninety-five north. I think Julie wanted me to call you."

"You think?"

"Yes."

"I'm getting in the car now. You can fill me in while I drive."

It hadn't been easy to convince him to come to Boston.

She told her father the computers at Systex Corporation had superior processors to the ones in Uzkapostan, which would enable her to hack into the Navy procurement database in half the time. That was a lie, but in Boston she had a fighting chance to save her own ass.

She was driving Leo's late model sedan down the interstate, the smell of old cigar smoke thick in her nostrils. Her father was in the passenger seat, a beer and a gun in his lap. The gun was for protection, he said, but Julie didn't believe him.

She'd watched that gun kill Leo, and it had probably killed Greg, too.

"Slow down. We don't want to get pulled over," he said.

That's what she was hoping for, which is why she was speeding. Easing her foot off the accelerator, she glanced in her rear view mirror to check for the minivan that had been following them since they left the house. Her father hadn't known Gwen was waiting outside for Julie, having shot Leo before the other man had a chance to tell him.

Call Hank. Tell him to come to Boston.

Julie was concentrating hard, and her head was beginning to pulsate in tempo with her own heartbeat. She was trying to send telepathic messages to her aunt for the last hour, feeling like an idiot trying to bend a spoon with her mind at a slumber party.

She didn't even believe in this stuff.

His business card's in my purse under the seat. Gwen, call Hank. We're going to my office in Boston.

Her father belched in the seat beside her. "I need to take a piss."

"I'll get off at the next rest stop."

"I gotta piss now. Pull over."

Julie knew she'd lose Gwen if she did that, and her grip tightened on the wheel. "It's the interstate, Dad. A cop might stop if we pull off the road."

He leaned in close to her, the stink of beer and unbrushed teeth permeating the air. "Just. Fucking. Pull. Over."

Julie put on her turn signal and felt Gwen's question as soon as she touched the brake.

Keep going, Gwen. Keep going.

As if in answer, the minivan swung around them, continuing down the road. Julie watched it disappear in the distance, leaving her completely alone with her drunken crazed murderer of a father, and a gun.

—10—

THE PRUDENTIAL TOWER stood sentry in the distance as Hank turned down Boylston and headed once again for the offices of Systex Corporation. The city streets were empty, the parallel lines of concrete sidewalks and asphalt streets dominating the landscape.

He couldn't help but feel he was going in circles, both literally and figuratively. Two visits to Boston. Two arson scenes. Chasing Julie south then north again. Chasing Julie even when she was standing right in front of him.

She was something else.

Hank rounded the corner and found the coffee shop Gwen had described, unlit except for its sign. The minivan idled at the curb and he pulled up behind it. Her willowy figure headed toward the passenger door.

"That was fast," she said, reaching for her seatbelt.

"I made up some time."

"Lucky you didn't get pulled over."

Hank pulled away from the curb and made a sharp left into the Systex parking garage. "Who said I didn't get pulled over?"

Gwen rubbed her hands on her thighs. "What's our plan?"

"Damned if I know."

He steered the car around the concrete pillars of the hulking structure, empty of cars at this time of night. "I'm hoping Julie left a way for us to get in."

"She might have."

"She better have." He pulled into the first spot after a series of handicapped spaces. Turning his body toward Gwen, he asked, "Do you know how to shoot a gun?"

"Yes."

He raised his eyebrows.

"I'm a country girl, Hank. I know how to shoot."

He nodded, handing her his backup. "We have to assume McDowell is armed."

"I think Julie's trying to tell me as much. I keep picturing a gun."

A fierce protectiveness surged through Hank at her words. The simple reality that she could be hurt released a torrent of energy. "Let's go."

An elevator next to the Systex Corporation sign marked the entrance to the offices. Hank stepped up and pressed the button, which lit beneath his hand. The doors opened and the pair stepped inside, neither knowing who or what they would be facing when the doors opened again.

"I NEED TO write some code to have my computer analyze the database encryption type."

"What does that mean?"

"I have to see what type of security they're using. I'm going to write a computer program to help me find out."

Julie sat down behind her desk and opened several windows on her computer. The first would make it look like she was writing the program for her father. The second would allow her to send text messages from her desktop to Gwen's cell phone. She set up her programs so she could quickly toggle between the two if her father came to look over her shoulder.

She typed, "IN MY OFFICE IN BOSTON. R U HERE?" Then she switched windows and began writing the computer program.

"This is where you work?"

"Yes."

"What do you do?"

"I'm the Director of Technology. I handle all the computer issues for Systex." Julie forced her eyes to stay fixed on the screen in front of her, though they wanted to seek out her father's face.

The man's a murderer and a traitor, and you're wondering if he's proud of you?

She swallowed her juvenile thoughts. "There's soda in the kitchen, just through there, if you're thirsty." Julie was certain he would have preferred something alcoholic, but she had neither the means nor the inclination to provide it.

He scratched his forehead with his thumb. "Coffee?"

"You can make some."

His brows snapped together, but he went in search of the machine. Julie flipped back to her texting program and saw that Gwen had answered.

"OUTSIDE MAIN DOOR. KEYPAD CODE?"

Julie felt the breath she'd been holding in her lungs release in a grateful huff. "568*14. STAY IN LOBBY. HAS GUN. KILLED LEO. SUNK DERMODY."

"R U OK?"

"4 NOW."

"HANK IS HERE."

Hank is here.

Julie made a little sob as she read the words.

"What are you doing?" said her father from the doorway.

How long had he been standing there? "Writing the program." She deftly toggled back to the other screen and hid the message from Gwen, though she could feel her cheeks burning a telltale red.

Her back stiffened as he walked behind her to see for himself, staring at the pitiful few lines of code that patterned the screen. It must have been enough to satisfy him.

"Where are the coffee filters?"

"In the cupboard to the right of the sink."

She counted to ten before walking to the door to make sure he was gone. Again she messaged her aunt. "CALL POLICE. GIVE THEM CODE TO GET IN."

It took several minutes for the reply.

"WILL DO."

Julie's shoulders caved in and her head fell to her chest. She had been in her father's company for nearly twelve hours. Her body and mind were fried from the constant state of high alert.

With a deep cleansing breath, she lifted her head and refocused her attention. She needed to get the gun away from her father so no one got hurt. She tried to predict how he would react, but her father was not acting like himself. Julie feared he would lash out at her as he had done to Leo and Greg.

For the moment, she busied herself writing what she hoped looked like a legitimate program, buying herself some time for Hank and the police to arrive. She managed to complete several screens full of computer code before the smell of burning coffee pulled her attention away.

Pushing her chair back from the desk, Julie prayed that everyone would be safe when this showdown was ended, then headed for the office kitchen.

"She wants us to call the police," said Gwen. They were standing in the lobby of Systex Corporation, the light from the EXIT sign highlighting the gloss on the tall black reception desk.

"The Navy should handle this, not local law enforcement." Hank rubbed the side of his index finger along his lip.

"I trust your judgment."

His eyes met hers. "I wish I knew who to trust."

"Barstow?"

"That's the question. The call should go to him."

"Hank, Julie says her father really was working for Uzkapostan. He was the traitor."

Hank's poised his thumb over his cell phone. "I believe her best chance of getting out of here lies with Barstow."

"That's all that matters now."

It was that simple, wasn't it? He loved her, and he would do whatever he could to get her out of here unharmed. For the first time, his decision had nothing to do with loyalty to the Navy or his own sense of right and wrong. He didn't care about anything except Julie.

"Barstow," answered the voice on the line, sounding no different at two in the morning than at two in the afternoon.

"We've got him, sir. I need backup at the offices of Systex Corporation in Boston, Massachusetts, ASAP. We have a potential hostage situation."

THE GUN WAS on the counter next to the coffeemaker, surrounded by a fine sprinkling of sugar that contrasted with the reflective black granite. She considered grabbing it, and imagined herself in control of the weapon. Could she turn it against her father to save her own life?

John McDowell was an imposing presence in the tiny kitchen. He stood at the sink, his back to her as he sipped his coffee and considered a piece of abstract artwork that hung between the two sets of wall cupboards. At fifty, his wide shoulders were still heavily muscled, his back graceful and catlike in its proportion and curvature.

"You'll never get there first," he said.

She swallowed against the tightness in her throat. "What?"

"The gun," he said, turning to face her. "You'll never make it to the gun before I do."

Julie stood up straighter and met her father's eyes fully. It was then, in the office kitchenette, that she was able to see him as he really was for the very first time.

The last mask had been removed, the final act performed.

John McDowell stood before his daughter, a man broken by hatred and his own willingness to allow evil into his soul. They squared off, each taking measure of the other, and Julie knew he would kill her as easily as he had killed the others. As soon as he realized she couldn't hack into the Navy's computers, she would be dead.

An unexpected freedom washed over her. She was not afraid. Suddenly able to distance herself from her father, she saw that her own achievements as a human being had surpassed the father she once adored. She was not beholden to him, but the victor in a battle that had been raging inside her since he left her alone in the world.

She needed only to placate him until the others arrived.

"I'm trying to help you, Dad."

"Of course you are."

The ring of the elevator arriving on the floor punctuated the silence, setting their tableau in motion. Her father reached for the gun with one hand even as his other came around her midsection, pulling her to him and placing the barrel of the pistol at her temple.

Julie fought him, writhing against the steel bands that were his arms. He ignored her attempts to free herself, dragging her toward the lobby where the elevator had surfaced and taking cover behind a tall potted plant.

The lobby was lit only by security lights, leaving areas of shadow throughout the waiting room and offices beyond. Julie's eyes raked through the familiar room, looking for any sign of Hank or Gwen. Had they been so foolish as to alert her father to their presence, or had the ringing of the bell been a deliberate distraction?

"Who knows you are here?" he hissed, the damp heat of his breath collecting in her ear. When she didn't answer, he snaked his arm across her neck and pressed painfully on her throat. "You double crossed me. This is how you treat your father?"

Julie fought for breath against the pressure of his arm, panicky in her search for air. A glass shattered on the wall next to them, and his arm yanked back in surprise. He pushed the barrel of the gun harder into her head and used her as a human shield, twisting and turning in an attempt to see the person who had thrown the glass.

From the corner of her eye, Julie glimpsed the doorway of the kitchen, dark against the lighter hallway. They had left the light on, she was sure of it. Someone was in there, the faintest silhouette of a human form hovering knee-high in the door frame.

So long as her father held a gun to her head, anyone who came to help her would be held as hostage as she. An odd calmness allowed Julie to consider her choices with a distant reserve. She could stay captive in his arms, or she could fight back.

Thrusting her weight to the right, her father's legs were forced apart as he tried to counterbalance her move. Her heel shot up quickly into the open space, connecting with his groin. His yelp of pain coincided with a loosening of his grip, and she pounded her elbow into his vulnerable solar plexus.

Her attention was focused on the kitchen doorway. She began to run, Gwen's silhouette now visible as her aunt got to her feet. Time slowed and the distance to the kitchen grew longer, moments held suspended as she waited for her father's inevitable reaction.

The walls pivoted around her and she knew she was going down, confused and panicked as her body began to fail her. Julie never heard the shots that entered her back and slipped into her chest cavity. The last thing she saw was Gwen's face, stricken in horror as her beloved niece fell to the ground, thick red blood seeping from the holes in her body.

—11—

"THE LAYOUT IS a square within a square," Hank said, recalling details from his initial meeting with Julie. "Offices on the perimeter, lobby in the middle, surrounded by an inner square of offices. Walkways from the lobby connect to the perimeter hallway."

Backup arrived fifteen minutes after he called Barstow, which felt like a fucking eternity. His muscles flexed as adrenaline flowed and he worked to keep himself in check.

"You're with me," Hank said to the tallest of the men. "You two take the other stairwell."

"I want to come, too."

He turned to Gwen. Anyone else, and he would have said no unequivocally. "Why?"

"I'll be needed."

He nodded. "Keep your gun ready. You are my

shadow. Stay a foot behind me, one hand on my back so I know exactly where you are."

She nodded.

Then they were moving, four flights dimly lit by security lamps and emergency exit signs, each of them on high alert.

Hank knew Julie was in danger. He could feel it in the marrow of his bones, as if the love he felt for her tethered them together on some cosmic level. Would she be alive by the time he got to her? The idea that he could lose what he had waited so long to find was incomprehensible. Would he be able to save her or was he already too late?

Pushing the thoughts away, he brought his focus back to the steady rhythm of his shoes on the stairs beneath him. The last flight came into view, ending at a single black steel door with the Systex logo in royal blue.

The team emerged silently onto a long corridor with brown industrial carpeting. Hank recognized it as the outer perimeter hallway. At the other end, two doorways spilled light into the darkness. Just then, a sliver of someone's head popped out and peeked in the opposite direction.

Was that Julie or McDowell?

The team inched forward, the men checking the offices along the way before giving the all-clear. It was a necessary step, but Hank itched to race toward the lit doorways, protocol be damned.

They were twenty feet from the same doorway when she emerged from it, walking away without ever turning in their direction.

Hank hesitated, unsure if McDowell would enter the hallway as well, when Julie turned into the second room. She was gone in a heartbeat, and so was his chance to alert her to his presence.

The smell of burned coffee reached his nostrils as he hovered close to the wall and inched toward the door. He heard McDowell's voice trailing out of what must be the kitchen.

"You'll never get there first."

"What?" It was Julie, so close. Right in the next room. His palms were hot and clammy, his eyes fixed on the doorway as he forced himself to take deep, slow breaths.

"The gun. You'll never make it to the gun before I do."

He's going to shoot her.

Hank's grip tightened on his weapon and he gestured to the men, holding three fingers up in the air, a countdown to action. He gave Gwen a shake of his head, telling her to stay put.

"I'm trying to help you, Dad."

He heard the stress in her voice, and knew that McDowell could hear it, too. Julie was running out of time. Two fingers.

"Of course you are."

One finger.

The ring of the elevator interrupted his countdown, unexpected and loud.

Hank froze and the men looked to him for direction. Sounds of a scuffle came from the kitchen, and Hank rounded the corner, weapon drawn, just in time to see McDowell exit the room from a door at the opposite end of the galley.

Julie was held securely against his chest in the classic hostage position.

"Gwen, stay here," he barked in a harsh whisper. "You two, take the perimeter hallway left. I'm going right." He jogged back the way the way he came, passing the stairwell and continuing on to the lobby.

Who the fuck was in that elevator?

The thought mocked him as he ran, heading toward a back entrance to the same lobby McDowell just dragged Julie into. He would have the advantage of surprise, though he had no idea what he would see.

Ten feet from the final turn to the lobby, gunfire exploded, one bullet for each of the three steps he took too late. He rounded the corner and watched Julie's legs bend and buckle under her lifeless form, collapsing at Gwen's feet.

A tortured howl ripped from his gut as he charged into the lobby, sweeping his gun from side to side in the shadowy space. The slightest reflection off the metal elevator doors caught his eye as they slipped silently together.

He fired his gun and the bullets embedded themselves into steel, never coming near their intended target.

The other men charged into the lobby from the opposite direction, weapons drawn. "He's in the elevator," barked Hank. "Split up and take the stairwells, now! I'll call for backup." They took off running at Hank's instructions. He dialed 911 as he rushed to Julie's side.

She lay on her stomach in a thick pool of black blood. He heard a rhythmic wet sucking noise, which he realized with horror must be her breathing. Gwen worked Julie's shirt up to see the damage the bullets had caused.

"I need an ambulance, quickly," he said to the emergency operator, giving him the address. "And police assistance. A fugitive has escaped from the same scene."

"I'M LOOKING FOR Julie Trueblood," Becky said, hearing her voice waver. "She was brought in by ambulance about an hour ago."

She had been in hysterics since Gwen phoned, and knew her eyes must be bloodshot as all hell. The woman behind the information desk gave her a sympathetic look, clearly used to seeing visitors skirt the border between life and death.

"She's in the ICU. Follow the signs to the blue elevators. It's on the fourth floor."

Becky swerved around people like pylons as she followed the blue ceiling tags to the elevator bank, only to find a crowd waiting for the next available car. She opened the door to the stairwell and bounded up four flights instead.

Not bothering to look for a reception desk, she grabbed the arm of a young man in scrubs. "I'm looking for Julie Trueblood."

A voice called out behind her, "Becky?"

She turned to see a man who looked weary with fatigue and stress, his clothing covered with stains that might be blood.

Too much blood to come from someone who was still alive.

"Are you Hank?" Her nostrils flared, eyes squinting as she approached.

"Yes. She's asleep, but you can..."

Her hand connected solidly with his face, a crisp clapping sound in the quiet of the hospital corridor.

"You were supposed to protect her!"

Hank cocked his jaw back into alignment. "I know."

"She trusted you to keep her safe, and now she's fighting for her life because you *did a shitty job of it*!" Becky glared at him, accusing eyes boring into his.

Hank met her gaze, seeming to accept her rage as just punishment. Then Gwen was there, holding her, telling her it was all right, which of course it wasn't.

"Come see her. She has lots of tubes sticking out, but she's still our Julie." Gwen put her arm around the younger woman and ushered her toward another tiled hallway.

"Is she going to be okay, Gwen?"

"It's too soon to say for sure."

"What do you think?"

Gwen squeezed Becky's shoulder and frowned a small smile. "I think we should hope for the best."

HANK STOOD STARING out the window, unseeing. The waiting room was angular and blue, full of squared-off metal chairs and rectangular couches, the people on them subdued.

He was giving the women time alone with Julie, but every moment he was away from her was its own special torment. McDowell was out there somewhere. Who's to say he wouldn't come here looking for the daughter he had failed to kill?

His cell phone rang in his pocket and he pulled it out to look at the screen.

He turned back to stare at nothing as he answered. "Jared."

"You are the biggest fuckup I've ever had the misfortune to command."

"Sir."

"Not only did you manage to let a notorious fugitive escape in the middle of downtown Boston, you allowed him to seriously injure a civilian."

"What do you want?"

The silence lasted so long, Hank was about to hang up.

"I want you to get back on track, Jared. This McDowell business is a goddamn train wreck, and you're the conductor. I'm shipping you out to Seattle. There's a case there…"

He interrupted. "I'm not going."

"Pardon me, son? *What did you just say?*"

"I said, I'm not going."

"I was under the impression you're an enlisted officer of the U.S. Navy."

Hank took the phone away from his ear while Barstow continued to speak. Snowflakes began to fall from the gray December sky and an image of Julie came to mind, standing on the church steps in her blue silk dress. Flurries swirled around her in the crisp night air.

Turning the phone over in his hand, he stared at the red button for several seconds before he pressed it, firmly. He was never one to do something without considering the ramifications of his actions.

BECKY STARED AT the thin layer of orange grease on the pepperoni pizza as the elevator stopped on each floor between the basement and the ICU. This time the wait didn't bother her, having seen enough of Julie's eerily still form tucked into a hospital bed to last her for a while.

The tray was laden with food, from Cobb salad and rice pudding to the pizza and a small turkey sub with American cheese. She sipped at a chocolate milkshake as the doors opened onto the fourth floor, and she went in search of Hank.

She found him at Julie's bedside, bent over in a chair, his forehead resting on the white sheet next to her hip. His hand held Julie's tightly, and Becky felt even worse for having attacked him.

He's in love with her.

He had changed into scrubs, the green color highlighting his bronze skin as it contrasted with Julie's pallor. But it was the way he sat, as close to her as he could be, that struck Becky most.

She considered herself to be an excellent judge of character, and she knew instantly that Hank Jared was a good man.

Crossing to the window, she curled up in a blue vinyl recliner and placed the tray on the table beside her. She was wrong to have said what she did, wrong to have slapped him. Her temper was fiery and explosive, often getting the better of her, but it was nothing compared to the remorse that typically followed.

Becky was a pro at apologizing.

The room was overly warm, hot and stuffy, a view of twilit Boston visible from the tall window next to her chair. She reached into her jeans pocket and retrieved a ponytail holder, quickly snapping her wild red locks into a loose bunch on top of her head to help her cool down.

She stared at the John Hancock building, her mind quiet. In the reflection of the hospital room, she saw Hank sit up and gently stroke Julie's arm from shoulder to wrist.

"I'm sorry if I woke you," said Becky, turning to face him.

"I was awake."

She noted the dark circles under his eyes. "When's the last time you slept?"

"Night before last."

"Gwen, too?"

He nodded.

"You can sleep at my house."

He looked at Julie, and Becky suspected he would not leave.

"Hank, I'm sorry."

He held up his hand. "Don't be. You were right."

"I'm sure you did the best you could." She reached for the tray. "I brought you something to eat."

His eyes took in the veritable buffet. "Just a little something?"

"I wasn't sure what you'd like."

"I could really go for a milkshake."

Becky's eyes went wide.

"I told you I wasn't sleeping."

Her eyes narrowed. "How'd you know it was a milkshake?"

"I can smell ice cream from forty paces."

"Harrumph."

Gwen walked in, her normally graceful posture now rounded and lax. "I spoke with the doctor."

"And?" said Becky.

"He says the next twelve hours are critical, but she seems to be holding her own."

"Thank God," said Hank.

"I need some sleep," said Gwen.

"You can sleep at my place. I was just telling Hank."

"I'll take the first watch," he said. "Go get some rest."

"Thank you, Hank. Ever since I lost David…" her voice trailed off and she grimaced, looking at the floor. "Hospitals are difficult. But I'll be back."

JULIE FELT LIKE she was swimming in thick water, unable to surface. She drifted in and out of consciousness as she paddled, her haze interrupted by vivid dreams and less tangible oddities from the world around her hospital bed.

She saw her mother standing in a field of tall grass, at once laughing and beckoning for her to come and play. At one point she could feel the hospital bed beneath her own still body and smell Gwen's favorite chicken soup, as if the woman were sitting beside her.

And there was Hank.

He wasn't with her in the water, but she could feel him somewhere near the water's edge. He wanted her to come out, but she didn't know how.

As she let herself drift in the current, she could smell his special scent and wished she could follow it. She could hear his voice.

"Please come back to me."

The love she felt for him swelled in her heart, making her buoyant in the water. She tried to move closer to him, deliberately pushing at the thickness around her with limbs that were tired and heavy. The water began to thin, becoming less fluid and feather-light, like a cool breeze.

She became conscious of her body, her closed eyelids. She worked to open them. The room was bright, sunlight streaming through the window onto the white sheets around her.

Hank held her hand, his unfocused gaze not realizing she was awake. She wanted to tell him, but speech was too hard.

This was a hospital room. Was she in an accident? She tried to remember what happened. An image of Gwen's stricken face emerged in her mind, and she saw herself fall to the ground.

Gunshots. There had been gunshots.

My father tried to kill me.

Panic had her suddenly jerking her arms up, her head moving from side to side.

Hank was there, touching her face. "It's okay, Julie. You're all right."

"My father?" she asked, her voice a dry rasp.

"Do you remember what happened?"

"Shot me."

"Yes. He shot you. The bullets punctured your lung, severed an artery. You're going to be okay."

"Where is he?"

Hank grimaced. "He got away." The terrified look on her face bored straight to his heart. "You're safe now, Julie. I promise. I won't let him get close to you again."

She nodded, tears welling in her eyes. Her own father had shot her with a gun, hoping she would stop living. The enormity of the thought defied comprehension. Looking back into Hank's eyes, she saw they were glistening and full of emotion.

"I let you down. I'm so sorry, Julie."

Julie shook her head as she reached up to stroke his

cheek. "Not your fault."

"Yes, it is."

"No, Hank." Forgiveness filled her eyes. "*His* fault."

He brought her hand to his lips for a kiss. "I love you, Julie." He looked into her eyes. "I knew it before, but I didn't say anything and I almost lost you. I'm not going to lose you again, and I'm not going to go another day without telling you how I feel."

"I love you, too," she whispered.

THOMAS BARSTOW STEPPED off the elevator onto the fourth floor and entered the ICU. He was dressed in khakis and a white polo shirt, an unremarkable choice. He met the eyes of no one as he strolled comfortably through the corridor and slipped into Julie Trueblood's room.

Two hours earlier, he called the front desk from a hospital courtesy phone and got her room number, then he waited in the lobby until he saw Hank leave the building.

He was virtually invisible.

It was always unfortunate when a situation required him to act directly. Whenever possible, he preferred to have others take care of the messier parts of his job. Still, the young soldier in him thrilled at the squeeze of adrenaline, the covert performance he was enacting on a live stage.

She was sleeping, and he took a moment to admire her simple beauty, so much like her mother's. It was ironic that her end would be at his hands, just as Mary's had been. Mrs. McDowell had been mere months away from death when he killed her, the cancer's havoc near complete when he learned she intended to name him in a lawsuit about the ionizing radiation at the worksite.

He couldn't allow that to happen.

Barstow walked to the head of the bed and examined the IV lines that entered the back of her hand, reaching into his pocket for the small glass vial and syringe.

"Hi."

The voice behind him made him drop the drug back against the lining of his pants. He turned to see a lanky redhead holding a cafeteria tray laden with desserts. He donned his warmest smile, the grandfatherly tone. "Hello there."

Becky stepped forward and put the tray down, eyeing him warily. "Who are you?"

He had only a moment to consider the question. "Tom Barstow," he said, offering his hand.

"Becky O'Connor." She scowled at him. "How do you know Julie?"

"I don't, actually. I'm Hank Jared's commanding officer." He carefully smoothed his features into an expression that exuded authority and trustworthiness, watching as she visibly relaxed in response.

They always do.

She picked up a macaroon. "What are you doing here?"

"I need to speak with Ms. Trueblood about what happened. I heard she's regained consciousness."

"Yes, but she's very tired."

"Of course. I wish it could wait, but with her father out there somewhere it's important that I speak with her as soon as possible."

Becky nodded. "Do you want me to wake her for you?"

"That would be good. Thank you."

Becky leaned in and touched Julie's arm. "Wake up, Jules. Someone's here to speak to you."

Barstow watched as she slowly opened her eyes. "Hank?"

"Hank went back to my place to sleep for a while. This man needs to talk to you about what happened."

He forced the breath in and out of his lungs despite his desire to hold it. Julie turned her eyes to his. As soon as they connected with his own, he knew he had made the wrong decision.

Julie Trueblood recognized him, and the last time he'd introduced himself, it was as someone else entirely.

12

THE TAXI LET Hank off in front of a Craftsman bungalow with green siding and red trim. He stepped out into the street under gray, stormy skies, careful to avoid the piles of slush and brown, melting snow. Digging in his pocket, he took out the key that Becky gave him and walked up the chunky front steps to the covered porch.

He unlocked the big wooden door and stepped inside, where he was greeted by a barking Pug. *Lucy? Lainey?* He couldn't remember what Becky said. The dog's scrunched black face and beady eyes contrasted with its sand-colored body and the mirth of its curled tail.

Stepping around the animal, he walked through the living room to the kitchen and helped himself to a glass of water. He leaned his tired body on the counter as he drained the glass.

"Ever since I lost David..."

Hank moved to the table as he pulled out his cell phone.

"Hank," answered Chip. "Did you find McDowell?"

"Yeah. Then I lost him again."

"Shit."

"Yeah." Hank rubbed his free hand down his face. "How're Melody and the babies?"

"They're great."

"She all right?"

"Uh huh. She's stable. Doctor says she's out of the woods."

Hank's head fell back. "That's awesome."

"What do you need?"

Julie Trueblood was shot by her father last night."

"Oh my God. Is she okay?"

"I think so." He closed his eyes. "Chip, the message you left the other day. David Beaumont."

There was a pause on the line. "I thought you didn't want to pursue it."

"I don't. But I can't stop thinking about it." Hank opened his eyes and sat back in his chair. "I mean, the guy was a music composer. What the hell does he have to do with *anything*?"

"I don't know. Do you want me to see what I can find out?"

"Yeah. Yeah, I do. But be safe. If it comes down to

it, it isn't that important. Got it?"

"Got it."

"Thanks, man. Give my love to Melody."

"Will do."

He hung up the phone and stared at the kitchen wall, unseeing.

Gwen was a special lady. If there was something to this, she deserved to know the truth.

BECKY STOOD OUTSIDE the nursery and watched a father cry over his newborn son. A nurse was checking the baby over and chatting with the dad as she moved her stethoscope over the baby's chest.

Becky had wandered off when Barstow wanted to talk to Julie, and found the hospital had little to offer in the way of entertainment. A quick spin through the gift shop yielded a coffee mug with "I love my Pug" drawn out in symbols and pictures, before a sign for the maternity ward caught her eye.

There were three other infants in the room, two girls and a boy, each wearing hand-knitted caps of pink or blue and swaddled in white blankets with pink and green stripes. As she watched, a woman in a bathrobe walked gingerly in, showed the nurse her wristband, and wheeled one of the girls out of the nursery.

Someday, that will be me.

Despite the pang of her biological clock, Becky was

in no rush to settle down. On the contrary, she enjoyed dating different men and not getting too attached to any of them. How could one man be as interesting as three or four?

At the moment, she was seeing a professional weightlifter, an architect, and a veterinarian, each of whom had qualities she liked. The vet was getting clingy, though, and she suspected she would need to let him go soon.

She looked at it like fishing for the perfect man. Catch and release, before they died in the bucket, or proposed marriage or something equally ridiculous. In the last three years, two men had proposed, and Becky was quite sure there was a distinct odor in the air at the time.

A little girl and an old woman entered the nursery hand-in-hand. The girl wore a pink T-shirt that said, "Big Sister" and the woman picked her up as they joined the man and the newborn boy.

Becky's heart constricted as she watched the father take the girl from the woman and introduce her to her new baby brother.

Oh, Meghan. I miss you so much.

A very young woman with raven hair, ivory skin and bright green eyes appeared in her memory. Older by nearly five years, Meghan O'Connor acted like a second mother to little Becky. She braided her long red hair, dressed her in pretty outfits, and took her for walks around the yard in the stroller.

As the girls grew up, they only grew closer, spending hours playing basketball, doing each others nails and telling secrets. At sixteen, Meghan was in love with Liam Wheaton, a strikingly handsome boy with strong features and dark brown hair. He was from the wrong part of town, with the wrong kind of family, and the girls' parents had forbidden Meghan to see him.

Young Becky had begun lying for her sister, so the couple could spend time together.

The last day Becky saw her sister, Becky was eleven. Meghan and Liam had taken her on a picnic in the country. There was a big field of golden grass and a small, shallow river where they spent the day wading and looking for crayfish.

"Always remember how much I love you, Monkey." Meghan was staring at her sister, the sunlight streaming through the trees behind her, making her look like an angel.

The next day, she and Liam were gone.

That was a very long time ago.

"Can I help you with anything?"

She turned to find a blonde-haired young man with piercing blue eyes and matching scrubs checking her out. Residents weren't usually assigned as hall monitors, and she suspected her veterinarian might be replaced by someone else with medical training.

"Hi." She put her hands in her back pockets. "I'm

Becky."

He tilted his head back and smirked. "Jim Hanguerer."

"Nice to meet you, Jim. Would you like to buy me a drink after your shift?"

He grinned widely. "I would love to."

"You're Barstow?"

This man looked like he had swung by for a visit between church services and a round of golf. The very idea of him being a threat to her was laughable, yet her stomach churned with anxiety at his mere presence.

"Would you excuse us please, young lady?" he asked Becky. When she was gone, he pulled a chair up beside Julie's bed and sat down. "I am. But you remember me as someone else, don't you?"

Her mother's last day on this earth, in a hospital room not unlike this one, a younger Julie returned from the chapel to find a stranger at her mother's bedside. He had introduced himself as Henry Goldstein. She wondered who he was to her mother, why he came to see her just hours before her death.

"Why did you lie to me?"

His lips pressed together in a firm line. "I didn't want you to tell your father I came to see your mom."

"Why not?"

"Mary and I were friends. She was the head engineer at a project I was overseeing at Camp Harold. Your father got the wrong idea."

A memory flashed in her mind, the family at a truck stop off the interstate, her father screaming at her mother in the parking lot, onlookers staring in shock.

"You were flirting with him. I saw you, damn it!"

So many times, so many accusations. Her father's rages were legendary, her mother's acceptance of his jealousy baffling to her daughter.

"I'm sorry he did that to you."

He nodded. "I got to say goodbye to Mary. That's all I cared about." He looked down at his hands, absently rubbing his fingers. "I still miss her, your mother."

"So do I."

"Taken from this world far too soon." He cleared his throat. "Anyway. I didn't come to talk about the past, I came to talk about what happened yesterday at Systex."

Julie walked him through the events of the last five days, though he already knew about many of them from Hank. He sat forward in his chair, never interrupting as she went through the details of her ordeal.

When she was finished, he bowed his head. "I'm sorry for all that you've been through, and I'm sorry I have to ask you this, Julie, but I do." He met her eyes with his own. "Are you sleeping with Hank Jared?"

She felt her cheeks heat at the intimate question,

feeling much as she had when the priest had caught her and Hank kissing in the basement. She looked at her hands in her lap.

"I see." He sat back in his chair, weaving his fingers together as he frowned. "I'd like you to break it off."

"What? Why?"

"You are the daughter of the most famous American traitor since Benedict Arnold. A lot of people—not me, mind you, but a lot of people—believe you were involved. It will destroy his career, Julie. Everything that young man has worked so hard to achieve."

"I haven't done anything wrong."

"I know that, but it doesn't matter. It's all perception. You are perceived to be the enemy, and Jared is perceived to be one who's sleeping with the enemy. He was going to be promoted to commander, Julie. Do you know how hard he's worked for that?" His eyes implored her. "That won't happen now."

Julie could feel her lower lip beginning to tremble and she bit down on it, hard. "But I love him," she whispered.

"If you really love him, you'll do what's best for him." Barstow leaned forward in his chair, his eyes beseeching. "I've worked with him for eight years, watching him persevere day in and day out for his career. He's a Navy man, through and through. It will break his spirit if that's taken away from him."

Was he right? Would Hank lose something that

was so important to him, for her? "I'll talk to him about it."

"You know what he'll say, Julie."

Yes, she did. He could be on fire, and he'd deny it if it would make her happy. Just a few hours ago, he told her he loved her and the world was at her feet. Now just as quickly, it was hanging by a thread.

"Maybe you can two can make it work after everything falls apart. I don't know. But I suggest you think long and hard before you make that choice, because you're making it for both of you."

Tears welled in her eyes and began to spill out over her lashes. "Where will I go? My father broke into my apartment once. I'm not safe there. Hank was taking care of me."

"I can protect you, Julie."

She stared at him, a dignified man with kindness in his eyes and an olive branch in his hand. He was her mother's friend, her lover's commanding officer. He would keep her safe.

Her head nodded in agreement, feeling the tears fall as she did. A gasping sob brought her hand to her mouth.

If you love something, set it free…

She cried until she fell asleep, a dreamless relief from the most difficult of days.

Hank didn't know what kind of flowers she liked, so he bought one of each.

A few hours of sleep had done him a world of good, and as he walked into Julie's hospital room he had a bounce in his step and a smile on his face.

She was sitting in the blue recliner, watching the rare winter thunderstorm rattle the city of Boston. The blanket of white had been ripped off the landscape by rain, leaving only shredded bits of snow smeared and diminishing in its wake.

"You're up," he said as he crossed to her, kissing her cheek. "That's terrific. How are you feeling?"

"Good. I'm good." She sat oddly still, her hands clenching the arms of the chair.

"What did the doctor say? Has he been in to see you?"

She nodded. "He says I'm going to be fine."

Hank offered her the flowers. "I brought you these. I wasn't sure what you liked."

"Thank you."

"Is everything okay? You seem preoccupied."

She looked back to the storm out the window. "I guess I am."

"What's going on?"

Lightning flashed and Hank found himself counting, waiting for the thunder. He got to five before she answered him.

"This isn't going to work."

Thunder crashed outside the window as shock glanced off Hank like a blow. He must have misunderstood. "What do you mean?"

"You and me. It's not going to work."

"Why the hell not?"

"I don't want to be with you, Hank. I'm sorry."

He stared at her unmoving body, her eyes never leaving his. The stillness that captivated her contrasted with mother nature's violent outburst outside. A different kind of storm took hold in his heart.

I'm not going to lose you again.

"You said you love me."

"I was upset. I confused gratitude with love."

"What, and the last six hours have cleared it all up for you?"

She looked away from him, another flash of lightning capturing her lifeless features.

"What happened between now and then, Julie?" He knelt before her on the tile floor. "Because I love you. I want to make a life with you."

She turned back to him quickly, her eyes angry and harsh. "I don't love you, Hank. I never did. You almost got me killed, you let my father escape. I'm lucky to even be alive. Now for God's sake, get the hell out of here."

Hank traipsed through the hallways, down flights

of stairs and got lost. A trash can beckoned and he threw away the flowers he had bought for the woman he loved. He was angry, he was confused. He was emotionally devastated.

Somehow he got back to his car in the parking garage, rammed the key in the ignition and started to drive. Where he was going, he had no idea.

The city streets were congested with traffic and he felt the world closing in on him. He picked up the ninety-three expressway and headed out of the city, quickly accelerating beyond the speed limit on the slick roads. He pulled his cell phone out of his pocket and dialed Barstow.

"You need to get a uniform on Julie Trueblood's hospital room."

"I thought you were taking care of that."

"Not anymore." He looked down and disconnected the call. He lifted his gaze and saw a family driving beside him on the road, reminding him that he was not the only one who might be hurt if he drove recklessly.

"Fuck." He said to himself, easing off the accelerator.

He ran his hand through his hair. What would he do now that Julie was gone? He had let her down, failed to protect her, and she couldn't forgive him. He understood that. He couldn't forgive himself, either. The knowledge burned at his gut like a physical pain. Julie Trueblood had every right to want him out of her life for good.

He just didn't have any idea what the future would look like without her in it. She had made him happier in a few days than anyone had made him in his whole life.

GWEN FOUND JULIE an hour later, propped in the same blue recliner like a lifeless doll. Outside the window, rain fell in a constant pour from the heavens.

"Julie, are you all right?"

Slowly her head pivoted to face Gwen. "Yes."

"Where's Hank? I thought he would be here?"

"I sent him away."

Gwen cocked her head to the side. "Why?"

"I didn't want him here anymore."

The healer in Gwen instantly wondered if Julie was suffering an infection. She walked over and put her hand on Julie's forehead.

"I'm not sick."

"Then what's going on?"

"What do you mean?"

"Why did you send Hank away?"

Julie frowned and shrugged her shoulder as if she had no idea of the answer. "I just don't think we should be together anymore."

Gwen sat down on the edge of the bed, close to her niece. "You broke up with him? What the hell is going on, Julie?"

Julie raised her eyes to Gwen's. "I'm not good for him, Gwen."

"Of course you are."

She looked at her hands in her lap. "I'm John McDowell's daughter. How do you think that's going to play at the office?"

Gwen pursed her lips. "I imagine it will be difficult for Hank at first."

"I imagine it will ruin his entire career."

"That's for Hank to consider, Julie. Not for you to decide for him."

Julie looked frankly at Gwen. "And what do you think he would say?"

"He would choose you, of course."

"Exactly."

"So that's it, then. You just sent him away." Gwen stood and walked to the sink, washing her hands and grabbing a paper towel. "I think you're being very selfish, Julie."

Julie turned wide eyes to her aunt. "No, I'm being very unselfish. I'm setting him free."

"You," she said, pointing at her, "are conveniently escaping a real relationship with a good man by bowing out gracefully at the eleventh hour. Shame on you, Julie. You're not even going to give him a chance, are you?"

"I'm doing this for Hank."

"Oh, bullshit, Julie." Gwen's chest heaved and her nostrils flared as she grabbed her purse off the bed. "You have a chance at happiness, my dear, that many people never get. Now, I'm going for a walk. I'll return when I am no longer angry enough to throttle you."

HANK GOT OUT of the cab, pulling his red and black carry-on behind him. The airport loomed wide before him, its curbside crowded with vacationers and businesspeople jockeying for position at makeshift check-in counters.

His uniform glittered in the midday sun, every badge and pin in perfect place, his shoes polished to a flawless shine.

The military was his life.

Barstow had called back, and this time Hank didn't hang up. He gave Hank orders to travel to Seattle for an investigation into the disappearance of two ensigns during a training exercise. It was a high profile case, and the admiral hinted that Hank would finally be promoted to commander if the investigation was resolved satisfactorily.

A family walked in front of him, husband and wife similar in height and build to him and Julie. Three small children followed behind, the oldest a girl, maybe five. She turned to Hank and waved, her other arm pulling a pink monster suitcase behind her.

He turned to walk into the airport, but his feet refused to move beneath him. A month ago, a year—he knew exactly what he wanted. Today all of those dreams were within reach. All he had to do was get on a plane and do his job.

But he didn't want those things anymore. He wanted Julie Trueblood.

Any other lieutenant could be standing where he stood, wearing the same uniform he wore, headed toward the same destination to perform the same job.

He turned in the opposite direction and gazed into the bright afternoon sun, shielding his eyes so he could make out the skyline of downtown Boston.

Julie.

Gwen had called this morning to let him know Julie had been discharged. She also asked him for a gun to give her niece, unable to obtain one herself on short notice. He proposed a trade—the weapon for Julie's address.

"I'm sorry, Hank. She wouldn't want me to tell you."

"And it's illegal for me to give a firearm to an unlicensed civilian."

The address was tucked in his lapel pocket. He pulled it out and knocked on the window of a cab as it began to pull away. "I need a ride," he said, climbing in as he loosened the collar on his uniform.

13

JULIE SAT ON the floor of the expansive room, the last bands of the setting sun streaming in through the floor-to-ceiling windows. Wood floors were stained a modern black, the walls covered in warm gold paint. An equally modern kitchen ran along the short wall adjacent to the windows, a hefty island and barstools rounding out the space.

Barstow had called her at the hospital this morning. "It was a textile manufacturing plant in the seventies. Being converted to loft apartments. This is the first unit that's come up for sale."

"Really, you don't have to…"

He cut her off. "It's an investment. You'll rent it from me, once you get on your feet. I'll have someone drop off the keys."

She had packed an overnight bag with the essentials, including a pillow and blanket. These she set up on the floor next to containers of Chinese take-out and a bottle of cheap Chianti from a liquor store down the street.

The only thing she put in the kitchen was the pistol Gwen had given her. It was in the drawer to the left of the sink, and in her mind it seemed to take up all the cupboard space and every square inch of countertop.

Isn't it just like Gwen to give me firepower?

Julie sipped her wine from a plastic cup as she let her eyes glide from one side of the space to the other, bumping up and over the square surfaces of the kitchen until they came to rest on the heap of her own belongings.

They didn't fit in here any more than she did.

Barstow's offer of protection seemed like a godsend at the time, but sitting in the emptiness made it clear that more had changed than her address. Hank was gone, and she was completely alone.

She had sent them away, of course. Becky and Gwen would never abandon her. A part of her needed this solitude, like an injured animal wandering away from the pack to lick its wounds.

The bottle in her hand was heavy with wine, and she rubbed her fingers against the woven basket that covered its smooth glass bottom. She loved these bottles as a child, their dark glass artfully drizzled with a rainbow of candle wax.

Tomorrow, she knew, she would move on without

even unpacking.

The gun from Gwen was a sign. She was in charge of her own protection now. Barstow was as unnecessary to her as the boxes of detritus Becky had so carefully hauled here from Julie's condo this afternoon.

None of it mattered without Hank.

Maybe she'd go south, just until it got warm, then rent an old house and plant a garden. Watch it grow. That would beat the hell out of the damn snow and ice and writing computer programs she didn't even care about.

The sun slipped below the skyline as Julie reached for the Chinese food bag. Two fortune cookies rattled in the bottom and she pulled them out, slicing open their wrappers with her teeth and slipping the papers from their crunchy folds.

Believe in love and it surrounds you.

She scoffed out loud—a bitter, desperate sound—and flipped to the second fortune.

Enemies and friends have similar features.

She thought of Barstow. He had been an enemy in her mind for so very long, only to be an ally in the end.

A loud clang of metal on metal came from the entryway and she started, adrenaline quickly shooting into her bloodstream. She slowly rose to her feet and strained her ears to hear, unable to see past an eight-foot high divider that separated her from the foyer space.

The silence that followed mocked the original clamor, and she fixed her gaze on the kitchen drawer some ten paces from where she stood. The path to the kitchen was visible from the doorway, and she hesitated, unsure of what to do next.

"Julie? Are you here?"

She exhaled the breath in her lungs, recognizing the admiral's voice. "Tom, you scared the shit out of me."

He walked into the space wearing a black leather jacket and aviator glasses, carrying a pizza box. "Sorry. I didn't think."

Julie watched as he put the box on the granite counter top and pulled out a cell phone, checking his messages. Crisp jeans landed on black leather boots, adorned with simple silver chains. She wouldn't have recognized him, were it not for his voice.

"You hungry?" he asked.

"I already ate. Chinese."

He shrugged out of his coat, revealing a gray T-shirt underneath. Julie was surprised by how muscular his upper body appeared in this outfit, compared to the polo shirt he had worn to the hospital. He turned back to the kitchen and began opening cupboards. Her gut clenched, thinking of the gun.

"Got any plates?"

"No, there's nothing."

"Oh, well." He picked up a piece of pizza and took

a large bite.

Julie tugged at the hem of her sweater. She thought he brought her pizza to be kind, but it looked like he was making himself comfortable on a barstool at the kitchen island.

Oh, please, go away.

She debated whether or not to offer him a glass of wine, neither wanting to be rude nor encouraging him to stay. Rubbing at the back of her neck, she decided rude was preferable. At least he might take the hint and leave.

An image flashed in Julie's mind, a picture of her firing the gun at Barstow. It was so real, more like a memory than anything, and it scared her. She looked beseechingly at the admiral. Was she losing her mind?

He met her eyes as he masticated, the muscles of his jaw working as he stared with eyes void of compassion. Gone was the affable and empathetic man who had visited her in the hospital, the stark contrast unsettling and dark.

Fear began to hum in her belly as the image returned. This time she could see the bullet entering his body, his head jerking back and to the side, blood splattering the taupe wall behind him. Her eyes traveled to look around the loft—failing to find any such wall.

"Would you like some wine?" she asked.

"Sure."

From her camp on the floor she retrieved her overnight bag, digging a bit before finding another plastic cup. She poured him Chianti and delivered it to his side. In one quick twirl, she caught the cup with her elbow and sent it to the floor, spilling its contents on his pant leg as it fell.

"Damn it to hell," he said, standing quickly.

"Oh, no. I'm so sorry," she said, hands splayed in mid-air. "There's a towel in the bathroom. You can rinse it out."

He stormed away, his body hulking from side to side like a much younger man. She positioned herself in front of the silverware drawer and waited until he was out of sight before grabbing the gun and tucking it in the waistband of her jeans.

Grateful for her bulky sweater, Julie pulled the yellow and green yarn down over the weapon and began to pour Barstow more wine. He reappeared the instant she picked up the bottle, making tiny beads of sweat pop out on her forehead.

"I am sorry, Tom. Did it come out?"

He walked up to her and grabbed her by the elbow. "How about we cut the bullshit, shall we?"

"What do you mean?"

In one move he reached his other hand under her sweater and pulled out the gun, then held the side of it against her nose. "Bullshit, Julie."

He pushed her away, making her lose her footing

and stumble onto the floor.

"You want to play games? Let's play a little truth or dare, shall we?" He worked to dislodge a piece of food from his teeth.

Julie got her feet beneath her, crouching on the floor beneath his imposing form. "Why are you here?" she said.

"Waiting for your father. I sent him a text message with this address an hour ago."

Her skin prickled hot and cold. "Why?"

"Oh, sorry. My turn." He was smiling like the Cheshire cat, clearly enjoying himself. "I dare you to stand right here in front of me," he gestured to the floor, "and tell me you haven't been in contact with your father in all these years."

It was ridiculous, but she felt her own desire to challenge him as she rose before him and raised her chin, speaking the truth. "I haven't been in contact with my father in ten years."

The slap met her face with such force, her head whipped around.

"Liar! The game is *truth* or dare. Nothing but a cunning little opportunist, just like your mother."

Hatred dripped from his voice, coating the words in ugliness. If he hated her mother, *why had he gone to see her in the hospital?*

Something clicked in her memory, a doctor in a white lab coat saying her mother would be going home tomorrow. Julie had gone to the chapel to give thanks for prayers answered, and found Henry Goldstein in her mother's room upon her return.

Thomas Barstow.

"You killed her!"

"She left me no choice." He raised arms at his sides. "She was going to name me in the lawsuit about the radiation. It would have destroyed my career, just like you are trying to destroy Jared's. The apple doesn't fall far from the tree, now does it?"

There was no statute of limitations on murder. Barstow had no intention of letting her walk out of here alive.

Too bad it's not his decision to make.

The courage roared up insider her, the will to fight for herself and win. She deliberately focused on the scene in her mind, Barstow's blood splattering on the wall. Confidence swarmed through her as she watched him fall, knowing that her premonition would become reality.

Her fingers itched to hold the cold metal of the gun, which rested on the granite next to his half-eaten pizza. Déjà vu wafted over her like a cloud shadowing the sun. She had already lived this moment in the kitchen of Systex, her father standing before her, her opportunity fading as she hesitated.

I will not hesitate again.

"This is so much fun. I've often dreamed of what it

would be like to talk to you. You're the only person who can really *appreciate* all that I've done."

Cold sweat lingered on her back, her underarms. "What else is there?"

He puffed his chest. "Pour me a glass of wine. And don't spill this one, you clumsy bitch."

She retrieved his cup from the floor and filled it, bringing the bottle back with her to the island. She took a seat at a barstool across from Barstow and her gun.

"Ah, these horrible little Chianti bottles with the baskets on them. Leo used to have them on every table."

"You knew Leo?"

"Of course. I introduced him to your father when I recruited McDowell to work for Uzkapostan." He swallowed half his wine in one sip. "We were quite a team, your father and I. I had access to information, he had the ability to decode it. It was un-fucking-believable what we were able to accomplish."

"Until the Dermody went down."

He nodded. "Our greatest triumph, but we were discovered when they traced the leak to my office. Fortunately for me, everything pointed to your father." He winked at her.

"But you were both guilty."

"No," he said, his eyes widening. "*We were both heroes.*"

He picked up the gun and twirled it around by the trigger guard. "Your father went back to Uzkapostan and everything was fine, until he started blackmailing me. At first I figured I was helping a comrade survive on the lamb. I knew your father wouldn't turn on me. But over the years he has gotten greedy. It is affecting my bottom line.

So I plugged the security hole in the Navy's procurement database, knowing he'd come out of hiding to get you to fix it."

"You've been trying to track him down ever since."

He nodded. "I almost had him that night at Systex. I threw the glass against the wall to try to separate you two."

"It was you in the elevator!"

He raised his glass. "Indeed."

"But he got away. So you gave him my address, hoping he would come after me, and you could get to him."

He pointed at her, a teacher to a star pupil. "Very good. Except he's not coming to get you," he began to laugh. "He's coming to protect you!"

Julie didn't understand. "He shot me."

"Your father didn't shoot you, Julie McDowell." His evil eyes glittered as he spoke. "*I shot you.*"

She saw him reach for the gun, but she snatched it off the granite first. Her hand clutched at the metal but failed to get a grip, the weapon dropping to the floor with a heavy rattle. Julie pivoted to retrieve it and Barstow kicked her away, picking up the gun himself.

She ran, her feet hectic as they worked to push her to safety, Barstow's footsteps thunderous behind her. She darted around one side of the barrier separating the loft from the front door and entered the darkened foyer.

Gunshots exploded just as she reached for the door handle.

A hundred and eighty pounds of weight slammed into her, propelling her into the steel entry door. Julie screamed. The body that crushed her fell to the floor, and she turned to see her father, blood streaming from his neck.

He had been hiding behind the wall, and deliberately placed himself between his daughter and her attacker.

"Daddy!"

His voice was a rasp, barely a sound. "Run!"

"Oh, that's so precious. A father rushing to save his daughter." The admiral clucked his tongue. "But it was all for naught, McDowell." He laughed hysterically. "Because you're blocking the door!"

Julie saw that he was right. Her father's body blocked her only escape. In that moment it didn't matter that she was trapped. All that mattered was that he had not tried to kill her, but had saved her instead.

"I love you, Daddy," she whispered. McDowell

took a final racking breath, then he was gone.

Barstow's cell phone rang and he checked the caller ID before answering it, the gun pointed at Julie. "What is it?" his smile turned to a scowl. "When?" He listened, then hung up the phone. "It seems your boyfriend's missed his flight to Seattle. I wonder where he could be headed?"

HANK STOOD ON the street outside the apartments, pacing. The door to the building was locked, with no way to ring the individual units. Alarm bells jangled in his brain as he phoned Gwen.

"No, it was definitely open this afternoon," she said. "Do you think she's all right?"

"No."

"I'm on my way."

"Call 911 first."

"I will."

He put the phone back in his pocket and strode to a bank of windows. He took off one shoe and used the heel like a hammer to break the glass, then clear away the shards. The opening was nearly three feet square, and he hoisted himself up and over the wall.

He was in a large empty room with a steel door at the far end. He jogged to it, threw back the lock, and entered a darkened hallway in search of the stairs.

A red exit sign led him to a stairwell, and he took

the steps two at a time as fast as his feet would propel him.

Becky's words tormented him as he climbed. *"It was your job to protect her, and you did a shitty job of it!"* Flight after flight he flew, breath coming in great gasping whooshes of air as he pushed his body to go faster, get there sooner, prevent what had happened from happening again.

Three deafening gunshots rang out on the other side of the fire door, half a flight from the seventh floor landing.

"Hank doesn't know where I am."

Barstow touched his finger to his chin and pursed his lips. "Now, why don't I believe that?"

"I broke it off, just like you told me to."

"That was excellent advice on my part. I had to extricate you from your bodyguard. Plus, I don't think he's ready to settle down, that one."

Julie's attention was drawn to the wall behind Barstow, which wasn't visible from the rest of the apartment. Unlike the honeyed gold that graced the other walls, this one was taupe.

There would be no Calvary, no knight in shining armor come to rescue her. Gwen had given her firepower, and though that gun was in Barstow's hands, the gift had little to do with the weapon. The universe raised its mighty sledgehammer and hit Julie Trueblood over the head with it.

Like a movie flashing in the darkness, she saw herself kneel before her father's body in grief, surreptitiously removing the concealed pistol from the ankle holster she knew he always wore. A warm feeling surged through her belly, and she knew her father would be happy it was his gun that would save the life he had died trying to protect.

She nodded her head slightly and allowed her lungs to fill with air. With more faith than she knew she possessed, Julie began to mimic the moves she envisioned in her mind. The emotions came of their own volition, first her face crumpling in grief. Her shoulders caved in around herself as racking sobs took her breath away, true feelings overtaking her as she allowed them to come freely to the surface.

Leaning over the body, *the last time she would touch this man*, she reached around his legs in an awkward embrace. She stealthily slipped the gun from its hiding spot beneath his trouser leg.

Barstow ordered her to stand up, as she knew he would. She bent at the waist, hiding the gun, until she nearly reached her full height and turned on him.

His face fell when he saw what she had found, his eyes hardening as he began to raise his own weapon.

Julie fired three bullets, each of them seeming to hang in midair. Barstow's head twisted at a horrible angle, blood splattering onto the wall behind him in a predetermined design.

He fell to the ground, dead.

The sound of his body hitting the floor was grotesque. For some moments she stared at his form, unable to comprehend what had happened. She looked up, gazing at the pattern of blood on the wall, realizing she stood in the presence of God. She fell to her knees.

Thank you for saving me.

Someone pushed the door behind her furiously into her father's body, and for a while Julie just watched. She heard Hank call her name, finally moving from her stupor to pull at her father's weight and allow Hank entry. He rushed in, his hands running up and down her body. Julie could hear sirens. She could see his lips moving, but she wasn't focused on the words.

For now, there was just the blood on the wall, the floor under her knees, and the awe in her exhausted spirit.

14

"I THINK YOU'RE a complete asshole."

Julie walked by her, carrying an armful of folded towels, and put them in the trunk of her car. It was already loaded with several turquoise duffel bags, a pillow and a worn lavender comforter. "You're entitled to your opinion, Becky."

She never did unpack the things she brought to the loft apartment, quietly nodding when the officer explained they would be tagged as evidence and held for at least thirty days.

Shopping seemed like a better idea.

Reaching into her jacket pocket, she took out her keys before letting the warm down parka slip from her shoulders.

"This is for you." She handed the coat to Becky.

"Don't go."

Tears threatened, fast and hot against her lashes.

"I'm leaving," she insisted, her voice a desperate rasp.

"Hank loves you. Hell, I love you."

Julie opened her arms and hugged her tight. "I love you, too." Slowly, she let her arms fall away from her friend. She climbed behind the wheel, numbly starting the engine. "I'll call you when I get where I'm going."

Red blotches mottled Becky's ivory skin. "I'll miss you."

"Enjoy that promotion. You deserve it."

She nodded, tears running freely down her face. "Drive safe, you stupid crazy bitch."

"I will."

Julie closed the door against the cold winter air and turned the key in the ignition. With a sad smile and a wave at her best friend, she pulled away from the curb and headed toward the interstate. Relief percolated through her mind, bringing with it the first real peace she'd experienced in what seemed like weeks.

After the incident, as she had come to refer to it, Hank had driven her to the police station in his SUV. He seemed to understand that she needed to be left alone. Julie was interviewed, and when she emerged she was grateful to find only Gwen waiting to take her home, a book of Sudoku puzzles in her lap.

"Hank said to tell you he loves you. He had some work to take care of in D.C."

And she knew.

The military was Hank's life, and it was the antithesis of hers. It was crazy to believe they could make it work.

She would be gone before he ever returned.

Moon Lake glistened silver in the morning sunshine, the Adirondack Mountains frozen in waves of purple and blue on the horizon. Hank pushed the lawn mower over his mother's rolling property, the noise from its engine drowning out all other sounds. The muscles of his arms and back reveled in the exercise, while his mind enjoyed the simple monotony.

Anything to keep from thinking about Julie.

He'd gone looking for her when he got back from D.C., only to find a For Sale sign in front of her condo. The dread in his belly clawed at his insides as he drove toward Becky's house, fearing he knew what she was going to say.

"She's gone, Hank."

"Where?"

Becky stood in the doorway of her bungalow, gazing at the horizon. "South. Someplace warm." She looked at her feet, then back at him. "I told her not to go. Actually, I told her she was an asshole, but she went anyway."

"Do you have a number for her? An address?"

"I do," she bit her lip, "but I can't give it to you, Hank. I'm sorry."

He stepped backwards away from the door, down the walk, reeling from the events of the last hour. When did she leave? Why hadn't he been here for her when she was making that decision? In his heart he believed he could have stopped her, convinced her to stay.

"Tell her I love her, Becky," he said, his throat knotted with emotion.

"She knows."

"Just tell her." He pivoted on his heel and headed back to his car, not knowing where he would go or what he would do. He only knew he would go out of his mind if he couldn't get to her, couldn't talk to her, couldn't touch her.

He finished mowing and released the safety bar, shutting off the engine. He pushed the mower back to the garden shed behind the house, finding his mother inside, potting up plants.

"Hey, Ma."

"Hey, yourself."

"Lawn's done."

"Thanks." She scooped a handful of potting soil around the bare roots of a hosta.

Hank rolled the machine into its spot next to the wall. "I'm going to Vermont."

"What for?"

He put his hands on his hips. "I'm going to ask Gwen for Julie's address. What's the worst that can happen? She won't tell me?"

Marianne put the pot aside and picked up an empty one. "It's about time, Hank. Give Gwen my love."

THE RINGING OF the doorbell set the dogs to barking as Gwen rolled the damp mass of spongy dough in cracked wheat berries. She set it in a wicker basket to proof, the final rise before baking on the stone she had heating in the oven.

She washed the flour from her hands and dried them on a fluffy red towel as she walked to the door. A warm spring breeze blew in through the windows, carrying with it the sound of wind chimes from the front porch. Gwen opened the heavy door to find Hank Jared standing with his hands in the front pockets of his jeans.

"Hi, Gwen."

A warm smile lit her face as she opened the screen for him. "Hank! Come inside." She opened her arms to him for an embrace of genuine affection. "It's good to see you."

"You too."

She walked into the kitchen, beckoning him to follow. "I was just finishing up some baking. Can I get you something to drink? I have some fresh iced tea."

"That would be great." It smelled like cookies as he walked into the kitchen and sat down at the island.

"You can probably guess why I'm here."

"Becky managed to hold out and not give you Julie's address." She reached into the refrigerator to grab the pitcher of tea. "She wasn't sure she'd be able to do it."

"I need to see her, Gwen."

"Yes, I know you do." She grabbed a couple of chocolate chip cookies from the cooling rack and put them on a plate in front of him. "To be honest, I expected you to contact me sooner."

Hank put both hands around his iced tea, looking into the glass. "When I found out she was gone, I thought there must be some misunderstanding. She wouldn't just leave without telling me where she was going. So I went to Becky's." He looked her in the eye. "That's when I realized she hadn't just left town, she'd left me."

Gwen looked into his deeply troubled eyes, her heart going out to him. He'd lost weight, but more than that he lost the warm glow that used to shine from his spirit.

"She's in South Carolina." Reaching into a tall cherry cupboard, she got herself a glass and filled it with the brew. "After she got out of the hospital, she spent one night at Becky's, then just packed up and drove away. I don't think she even set foot in her old condo, except to get her cat. She called a woman who does estate sales and a Realtor and that was that."

"Can I have the address?"

She nodded, taking out a fabric address book from a drawer and copying it onto a small sheet of paper. She held it out to him.

"Be patient with her, Hank. I love her more than anyone, but running away is the only way she knows how to deal with her problems. Julie has never learned how to stay."

"Well then, I guess I'll have to teach her."

"I wish you luck, my friend," she said, smiling warmly.

Hank reached out and pulled her close for another hug. "Thank you, Gwen."

"Take some cookies. It's a very long drive."

JULIE STOOD IN the sunny yellow kitchen cutting slices of avocado, an orange tiger cat purring at her feet. A vibrant plate painted with red and blue daisies was laden with salad greens, its edges chipped from age. She added chunks of blue cheese and crumbled bits of bacon strips, haphazardly covering the pile with pieces of hard boiled egg and cold grilled chicken.

Grabbing a pitcher of freshly squeezed lemonade, she headed out the kitchen door and onto the screened porch, the humid air instantly covering the smooth glass with a fog of condensation.

This house had been a haven for Julie, a small

painted lady with a pinky-red exterior and yellow shutters. The porch overlooked a lush garden bursting with plump vegetables, and a glorious weeping willow she imagined had been planted by the original owners.

She filled her days walking in the sun, weeding her garden, or reading on the porch. It was only at night that the dreams of him came, sure as the moon rose into the sky. She lay in his arms, desire a living, breathing animal with a will of its own. Steeped in his scent, she surrendered to her lover once more, every touch marking her his, every emotion connecting their spirits.

With the sunrise and consciousness came a rededication to live without him, to keep her tears inside, to plan a future without Hank Jared. Some days, she even thought it was possible.

She sat eating her salad, swaying in a white wooden rocker, unaware that some bites had more chicken, others too much egg. She didn't move when the doorbell rang, assuming it must be a delivery man or solicitor, and not caring to engage either one.

"Julie."

He was standing at the corner of the house, next to the white rosebush. She stopped rocking and stared at him, shockingly handsome in khaki shorts and a fitted polo shirt. She hastily finished chewing the salad in her mouth and set the bowl aside, slowing rising.

"I couldn't stay away." He took a step toward her.

"I tried to, but I missed you so damn much."

Emotions came raging to the surface, choking her. She covered her mouth with her hands. He moved more swiftly now, covering the distance that separated them, coming onto the porch, his eyes never leaving hers. Then he was there, his arms around her, her face pressed into his neck, his scent surrounding her.

"Oh, Hank."

He stepped back, holding her face in his hands and watching the emotions play over her features. "Don't leave me again, okay?" She nodded as he covered her face with kisses. "Don't do that to me. We belong together."

He bent his head to hers as she reached for him, their lips meeting and melding, becoming one. Her arms clutched at him, pulling him tighter against her body as heat surged through her belly, fluid and warm.

She led him into the house, up the stairs to her bedroom.

Everything she had run from reared to life inside her, the fervent hopes and dreams of this love, of this man, coursing through her body. She opened herself to him, her mind and soul, allowing the love she felt to flow freely, uninhibited and proud.

There was a truth between them that was remarkable and strong despite their separation, and she reveled in their passion, seeing for the first time that their love for each other was honest and good, and could see them through the darkness.

Hank Jared was meant for her, like a flower was meant for the sun.

And she knew. She was going to hold on to this man forever.

JULIE CUDDLED UP to Hank's back and threw her leg over his. They had been making love and sleeping, on and off for the past twelve hours.

"I don't even know where you live," she said, giggling.

He cleared his throat. "With my mom."

"You do not."

He turned his head into the pillow. "Actually, at the moment I do."

"Why?"

He rolled onto his back, lifting his arm for her to snuggle closer. "I used to keep an apartment in D.C., but I wasn't there enough to say so. I gave it up when I resigned my commission. Then I couldn't bring myself to get another place without…"

She interrupted. "When you *what?*"

"Resigned my commission. I left the Navy, Julie."

"What? When?"

"When I went to D.C. for my debriefing after Barstow died."

She sat up, pulling the sheet up to cover herself.

"Because of me? They made you resign because of me?"

"They didn't make me resign. I quit."

"But why?" She waved her hand at him. "You love the Navy. The military's everything to you!"

"No, Julie. *You are everything to me.*" He caressed her cheek. "The Navy was just a job."

She threw the blankets back and strode to the bathroom.

"I did it to make you happy," he yelled after her.

She stomped back into the room, tying a light blue robe around her waist. "Well, why the hell didn't you ask me first? You just go and quit the Navy like it's freakin' Burger Hut and expect me to be grateful?"

He put his hands up. "Wait. What's happening here? You hate the Navy. You couldn't stand that I was an officer. Does any of this ring a bell? You didn't want to be involved with me because of the Navy."

"I didn't want you to quit, Hank."

"I got that. But I don't understand why."

"Forget it. Just forget it." She paced the room. "I don't want to talk about this right now."

She turned and headed for the porch, the cool night air smelling of rain. She sat in her rocker, mentally daring him to follow her. When he did not, she let her shoulders drop and took a deep breath, the pungent smell of honeysuckle only now permeating her awareness.

The buzzing of cicadas mixed with the chirp of frogs and the steady rhythm of her rocking chair. Her body cooled along with her temper, and she began to feel sorry for fighting with Hank.

How could he think that leaving the Navy would make her happy? She didn't want him to give up what he cared about. Her father was the traitor, the murderer and the psychopath. It was her problem, and she should be the one to pay the price for it. Not Hank.

An hour passed before she saw him standing in the doorway, and she stopped moving.

"May I join you?"

She nodded.

He sat in the wooden porch swing across the way, his muscular arm draped across the back in artful silhouette.

"I'm sorry I got so upset," she said.

"Can you explain it to me?"

She set her chair to rocking. "I don't want you to sacrifice something you love for me."

He was quiet for a moment, and she waited to see what he would say. "Why not?"

"It makes me uncomfortable."

"Julie, that's what people who love each other do."

"No, it isn't."

"Sure, it is. They sacrifice and they compromise, they bend over backwards to make each other happy. That's what it means to be in a committed relationship."

He made it sound so rational, so reasonable. She had never been in love before. Her parents had never gone to such lengths to make each other happy.

Okay, bad example.

Her eyes began to burn as the truth made its way to her lips. "I don't deserve it."

He was up in an instant, kneeling before her chair, grabbing her hands and holding them in his own. "You do," he said, kissing each palm. "And if you'll let me, I'll spend the rest of my life trying to prove it to you."

She leaned over, her forehead resting against his as she cried. Was it possible that this incredible man knew everything about her past, and loved her anyway?

"Will you let me, Julie? Let me show you how much you deserve it, how much we both do?" He reached up and gently put his hand on her neck. "Will you be my wife?"

"I'm not good at this, Hank. I don't know what a healthy marriage looks like."

"We'll learn together, Julie. We'll figure it out as we go."

All the women in the world, and he wants to marry me.

A sob escaped as she nodded. "Yes, Hank. Yes, I'll be your wife."

ABOUT THE AUTHOR

Amy Gamet is a former teacher turned stay-at-home mom.

She lives in New York State with her husband and children.

Meant for Her is her first novel.

Author updates can be found at www.amygamet.com.